DEAN R. KOONTZ
ODDKINS
A FABLE FOR ALL AGES

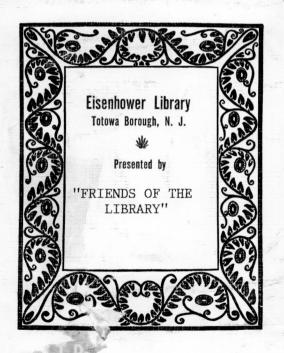

PARKS

CREATED BY CHRISTOPHER ZAVISA

WARNER BOOKS

A Warner Communications Company

The perpetrators of this book dedicate it in the following manner:

DEAN:
To Gerda, who makes every day of my life a day of childlike wonder.

PHIL:
To the late Herbert J. Parks, who—with my mother—saw my world on paper... and approved.

CHRIS:
To Gail, Nicole, and Zachary, who see the same magic in the world that I see.

Copyright © 1988 by Nkui, Inc., Airtight Graphics, and The Land of Enchantment
All rights reserved.
Warner Books, Inc., 666 Fifth Avenue, New York, NY 10103

A Warner Communications Company

Printed in the United States of America
First Printing: October 1988
10 9 8 7 6 5 4 3 2 1

Interior design by Elaine Groh

LIBRARY OF CONGRESS
Library of Congress Cataloging-in-Publication Data
Koontz, Dean R. (Dean Ray), 1945–
Oddkins/by Dean R. Koontz; illustrations by Phil Parks; based
on an idea by Christopher Zavisa.
Summary: When the death of their creator leaves them without protection, a band of magic living toys must attempt a dangerous
journey across the city to another toyshop, while under attack from evil toys serving the Dark One.
[1. Toys—Fiction. 2. Fantasy.] I. Parks, Phil. ill. II. Zavisa, Christopher. III. Title.
PZ7.K83570d   1988
[Fic]—dc19   87–27987   CIP   AC
ISBN 0-446-51490-X

ODDKINS

1

A Very
Dark Day

1.

Amos the bear was standing on the toymaker's bench, looking through the casement window at the purple-black storm clouds rolling in from the east. He was filled with great sadness—and fear.

This is a dark day, he thought, and he shivered.

Stripped of leaves, the November trees were stark, like many-armed black skeletons. The red light of the setting sun was fading fast. Soon night would fall, and it would be very dark. The oncoming storm would blot out the moon and stars.

To Amos, it seemed as if dawn might never come again, as if the world would forever turn in deep gloom.

The day was grim not merely because of the weather but because Mr. Isaac Bodkins, the toymaker, was dead. To his creations, the magical stuffed-toy animals that he had called Oddkins, he was "Uncle Isaac," and they were deeply saddened and frightened by his passing.

For many weeks the old man had known that he was dying. But the end had come quicker than he had expected. This morning, feeling tired, he had decided to lie down on the couch in one corner of his workshop, just to rest for half an hour before lunch. He had passed away peacefully in his sleep.

Sam Jenkins, who owned a toy shop and sold Isaac Bodkins's creations, had come to pick up some merchandise and had discovered that the old man's sleep was deeper than it should have been. While all the stuffed toys sat on shelves and workbenches, pretending not to be alive, Mr. Jenkins called the doctor. The doctor came, carrying a bag filled with instruments and medicines. Seeing the physician, the Oddkins had felt a surge of hope. But eventually Uncle Isaac's body had been taken away.

Now the stuffed animals were alone in the rambling old house that had been Mr. Bodkins's workplace and home. It was still the home of Leben Toys, the beloved old man's small company. Grief was so heavy in the air that Amos the bear felt it pressing on him, making his shoulders sag.

He would have wept if he could have formed tears. With his great skill and magic Mr. Bodkins had given life to the toys he made. But Amos was still only a teddy bear, after all. He could not produce tears, no matter how much he ached to shed them.

Behind Amos, in the workshop, the others sobbed. Like him, they were unable to weep, but they could make the soft sounds of grief.

Amos would not permit himself one sob. He must be strong, for Uncle Isaac had chosen him to lead the others in this terrible time.

Last week, Isaac Bodkins had taken Amos into the book-lined study at the front of the house, where they could have a private conversation. The toymaker had sat behind his richly carved desk while Amos had sat on top of it, basking in the red-yellow-blue-green light from a stained-glass lamp. The old man had talked about Amos's destiny and had revealed certain secrets. . . .

Leaning back in his big leather chair, Uncle Isaac folded his aged but still strong hands on his round belly. Peering at Amos over the tops of his tortoise-shell glasses, he said, "You know the reason you were made, of course, the reason I've made all of you Oddkins . . ."

Amos sat up straight and proud. "Oh, yes, sir! One day I'll be put on display in a toy shop. I'll be sold as a gift for a very special child who'll desperately need a secret friend."

"That's correct." Mr. Bodkins smiled and nodded approval. "It will be a little girl or boy who, if he grows up whole and happy, will contribute something of importance to the world. A special child, as you have said. But this will be a child who has to face enormous problems or who must live through a terrible sorrow. Perhaps it will be a child whose parents mistreat him—"

"Or maybe one who'll fall ill and need tremendous courage to pull through," Amos said solemnly. "Or a child whose mom or dad dies . . . or who loses a sister."

4

"Yes. But whatever the child's problems, you will be there to offer comfort, counsel, and love. You *must* help the child to grow up confident and loving, regardless of what cruelties the world inflicts on him. Because, you see, this special little girl or boy of yours will perhaps become a doctor who saves lives, or a diplomat who negotiates peace, or a teacher . . . if only he can grow up whole and happy. But if he's broken by the tragedies he must endure, then he will never have a chance to make this world a better place."

Sitting on the desk in the multicolored light of the stained-glass lamp, his furry legs straight out in front of him, leaning back on his forepaws, Amos sighed heavily. "Gosh, it sure is a big responsibility."

"Enormous," Mr. Bodkins agreed. "And you must always remember that you and the other Oddkins have to conceal your missions from everyone—except, of course, from each other and from your special children. In the privacy of that boy's or girl's room, you'll be alive, but to the rest of the world you must pretend to be only a stuffed animal."

"I'm good at that," Amos said happily. He went stiff, and his eyes were suddenly as blank as painted buttons.

"Very good," Isaac Bodkins said. "Excellent!"

Amos grinned, and his eyes became expressive and warm again.

"If you let another child or any adult see your magical life, you won't remain effective as a secret friend to your assigned child."

"Yes, sir," Amos said. "I understand."

It was also understood that, once his assigned child's crises had passed, when a secret friend was no longer needed, the magical life would drain out of Amos, as it went out of every Oddkin sooner or later. Then he would be only a teddy bear, just like any other. In time, his special child would forget that Amos had once *really* been alive. Their secret conversations and adventures would seem to have been fantasies, mere games that the child had played in more innocent days before growing into the no-nonsense world of adults.

This fading-away of his life was a difficult thing for Amos to accept. But he understood that true magic was strictly for children and would only confuse and upset most adults. Many people had been guided by one Oddkin or another in their troubled youth, but none of them remembered the truth after they grew up.

Amos rose and walked around the stained-glass lamp, stepping over the cord, frowning at the gleaming oak desktop. "Something I've been wondering about," he said in a gruff voice which should have seemed too deep for his small body but which strangely fitted him. "What happens when the life goes out of me, Uncle Isaac? Do I have a spirit? Does my spirit go to Heaven or someplace? What happens to me? Is *that* one of the secrets you've brought me here to tell me about?"

Isaac Bodkins shook his head. His fine white hair gleamed like moonlit snow. "No, I can't tell you that, dear Amos. What comes after life must remain a mystery to you, just as it is a mystery to human beings . . . including me."

Even then Amos had known that Uncle Isaac was dying. The old toymaker had not hidden his illness from his creations. In fact he had encouraged them to get used to the idea of his passing. A new magic toymaker must be chosen during the next few weeks. And when Isaac Bodkins died, those Oddkins who were still in the shop would have to help the newcomer settle into his job.

A few days ago, when Uncle Isaac told them that he, their maker, would soon trade this world for another, the Oddkins had pretended to be strong and stouthearted. They pretended to accept his approaching death with regret and sadness but also with grace and courage.

In reality they were sick with grief—and scared. Very scared.

"Death," Uncle Isaac had told them, "is not an end. It is only a station between two places. There's a new beginning beyond death. Don't be afraid for me. I'm merely going on to a new life of some kind that I can't imagine but that I know will be even better than the life I've had here."

"But we'll miss you," Butterscotch the dog had told him, unable entirely to conceal her misery.

"And I'll miss you," he said. "But I will never forget you. In memory we'll always be together."

"Memory?" Skippy the rabbit had said scornfully, brash as usual. He had cocked his head in the direction of his floppy ear, as if it were pulling him over on his side—the other ear was straight—and he had squinted at the toymaker. "Memory's not good enough. Memory fades—"

"Mine doesn't," said Burl the elephant.

"Well, Mr. Hose Nose, everyone *else's* memory fades."

"Too bad everyone isn't an elephant," Burl said.

"Heaven forbid!" Skippy declared. "If elephants were the only creatures in the world, they'd have eaten everything down to bare rock and would've died out long ago. Walking stomachs, that's what elephants are. And can you imagine the *din* of all that trumpeting, the thunderous pounding of all those billions of big feet?" Before Burl could respond, Skippy had looked at Uncle Isaac again and said, "No, sir, having you in memory isn't good enough by half."

"I'm afraid it will have to be good enough," Mr. Bodkins had said quietly but firmly.

And now, in his study, he was equally quiet and firm with Amos. "Worry about *this* life, Amos. Worry about doing well in this world. The next world, whatever it is, will take care of itself."

Though he was only a stuffed-toy bear, Amos had a good, solid bearish personality. He was slow to become excited, and he was patient, and he tended to think about all the possibilities before acting. So he stared at Uncle Isaac for a while, finally nodded, sat down on the desk blotter, and said, "Okeydoke," which was his way of saying, "All right, okay, I'm agreeable to that."

Leaning forward in his chair, closer to the lamp, Isaac Bodkins said, "But I *will* tell you the meaning of the symbol on your sweater."

Amos's eyes widened. "You will?" Ever since he had come alive on the old man's workbench a couple of months ago, Amos had wondered about the mysterious symbol on his blue sweater. "Will you really tell me?"

"Alpha and Omega," Uncle Isaac said.

"Huh?"

"That means 'the first and the last.' "

Frowning, Amos said, "The first and last what?"

Uncle Isaac leaned even closer, until his kind face was like a moon hanging low over Amos's world. "After I have passed away, there may be a time during which the new toymaker is not fully in charge. After all, it takes a while to accept the mantle of magic and to feel comfortable with it. During that time, when the new toymaker is not totally in control, there may be . . . trouble, danger. . . ."

"What kind of trouble? What danger?" Amos asked, his pleasant furry face settling into a bruin's scowl.

Isaac Bodkins hesitated. Then he sighed. "You'll know it when it comes. And then you'll be first among all the Oddkins, the leader of them in any time of crisis."

"Me? Leader? Hmmmmm. I'm not sure—"

"Yes, you can lead them, Amos. I *made* you a leader."

Pride surged through Amos, and he sat up straighter, puffed out his chest. He considered what Uncle Isaac had said, then nodded. "All right. I'll lead them. You can count on me."

"You will be the first to confront trouble."

"Yes, Uncle Isaac, I will," Amos said, though he had no idea what sort of trouble he might have to confront.

"And you will be the *last* to turn away from it."

Amos stood, squared his shoulders, and nodded.

The wire rims of the old toymaker's glasses glinted with orange light from the stained-glass lamp. Spots of blue and green and red were reflected in one lens. In spite of this cheerful coloration, Uncle Isaac was somber, not like himself at all. "In bad times, you will be the first to give heart to your friends—and the very last to be dejected. You'll be first in courage and the last to be afraid."

"Me?" Amos said, blinking. "Afraid? Not me. I'm not afraid of anything. No, sir. Not me."

"But there are things in this world that you *should* be afraid of, Amos."

"I should?" Amos asked uneasily.

"And if you encounter them—*when* you encounter them—you'll feel the cold grip of fear."

"I will?"

"But you must be the last to give in to it."

"I promise," Amos said.

That had been less than a week ago. Now as Amos the bear stood on the age-worn workbench and stared out at the oncoming storm and at the descending twilight, he felt gripped not only by grief but by that cold fear. Uncle Isaac Bodkins was dead. The old man had thought he had a few weeks of life left. But now he was gone, and things that should have been done before his passing—such as the choosing of the new magic toymaker—remained unfinished.

Lightning flickered along the edges of the clouds. The fiery red sky in the west had turned purple-red and would soon be dark.

Amos turned from the diamond-paned casement window and surveyed the big workroom. Ordinarily, in spite of its size, the shop looked warm and cozy. The walls were cream-colored, hand-textured plaster. The floor and the beamed ceiling were of lustrous dark oak. The many tool and supply cabinets were also of oak, to which Mr. Bodkins had added beautifully hand-carved decorative vines and leaves and birds. But today, a damp chill reached into every corner of the room.

The other Oddkins grew quiet when Amos turned from the window and faced them. Fifty-one of their magic kind were gathered in the workshop, the only ones who had not been sent off to toy shops before Isaac Bodkins's death. There were teddy bears, though none like Amos, for each Oddkin was different from any other. There were dogs—a Dalmatian, a spaniel, a golden retriever, a Scotty, and more. Two velvet penguins. A lion with a mane of yarn. A duck. Three cats.

They stood in small groups on the floor below Amos, or huddled singly in corners. Some perched on the tops of supply cabinets, looking down at Amos, while others sat in stunned silence on the sofa where Uncle Isaac had passed away in his sleep only hours ago.

"I dropped the 'B' from 'Bodkins,' added another 'd' after the 'o,' and called you 'Oddkins,'" Uncle Isaac had explained to Amos, "because you are my *kin* in a way, my only children. And let's face it, you're all a bit odd, aren't you, my furry little friend? Odd kin. You are my wonderfully odd children. I love you all."

Amos swallowed a moan of grief and jumped down from the workbench to the stool on which Uncle Isaac had sat when stitching together his wondrous creations. From this slightly lower perch, he addressed the assembled toys: "We have a difficult and dangerous mission to perform, and we must act tonight."

2.

Two floors below, in the toy factory's secret subcellar under the known cellar, all was dark and still and musty as it had been for many decades.

Then light appeared. No one had turned it on. It just *came* on of its own accord, or as if a ghost entered the chamber and flicked a switch.

At first, it was not much of a light, dim, like the pale glow of a winter moon reflected in snow and frost. Most of the deep, deep cellar was still cloaked in thick gloom. Nothing could be seen except a small section of cobblestone floor and stacks of old wooden crates.

CHARON TOYS was imprinted on every crate, for that was the name of the company that had occupied the toy factory before Isaac Bodkins had founded Leben Toys. These boxes of various sizes were festooned with cobwebs. Their lids were hidden by inch-thick blankets of dust.

Something thumped.

Something creaked.

Suddenly a shiny blade poked through the crack between the lid and the side of one of the crates. Something within the box was prying its way out. Wood splintered with a dry sound. An old nail began to pull loose with a series of sharp squeaks.

A disturbed spider scuttled down a trembling web and vanished into the darkness.

The gleaming blade moved along the crack inch by inch, prying at the lid, and one by one the nails pulled loose. Then the lid was thrown back, and Rex emerged from the crate that for decades had been his coffin.

Rex was a tall, slim marionette, but at the moment no strings were attached to him. He was dressed in black shoes, a black tuxedo, a black top hat, white vest, white shirt, white tie, and white gloves.

His eyes had a cold, wild look as he slowly surveyed the shadows around him.

The marionette's white garments were slightly soiled with faint gray and yellow stains. His tuxedo was filmed with dust and faded in places. The right shoulder of the coat had been eaten away by moths, so the upper part of his jointed wooden arm showed through. The red silk carnation in his lapel was rumpled, tattered.

Cobwebs wound around him as he had climbed from the crate. He brushed them off his coat sleeves and trousers.

He smiled, but there was no humor or warmth in that smile. His lean, cruel face was painted like a stage actor's: pale except for spots of rouge on both cheeks, penciled eyebrows, and bright red lips.

"Alive," he said, and his voice echoed eerily through the shadowy subcellar. "At last, alive again."

He carried a sleek black cane that had a straight rather than curved handle, the cane of a stage dancer rather than that of someone truly in need of support. From the tip, a gleaming steel blade protruded. When he touched a button on the handle, the knife snapped back into the shaft of the cane, entirely hidden.

The dim bluish-white light from the stained-glass chandelier gradually began to brighten. Farther away in the vast room, another chandelier came on, and it too grew slowly brighter.

The deep cellar seemed like a living creature that was finally awakening after a long sleep.

Rex laughed. It was a cold, mean laugh.

Unlike the Oddkins two floors overhead, Rex was not a good toy.

3.

Still addressing his fellow Oddkins from the workbench stool, Amos the bear said, "This morning, Uncle Isaac decided who should be the next magic toymaker. He chose Colleen Shannon. She owns the toy shop in the city."

"She's nice," one of the velvet penguins said from the sofa on which he was sitting with a cat, a dog, and a squat green frog.

"I like her," Burl the elephant said. He was a stout fellow who wore a white shirt with the sleeves rolled up, a fawn-colored vest, and dark brown pants held up by suspenders. "I like Mrs. Shannon very much, as much as I'd like peanuts if I were a real elephant and could *eat.*" He lifted his floppy ears slightly and gave a short side-to-side wave with his trunk, as if underlining his statement.

The other Oddkins murmured agreement.

"Uncle Isaac was going to invite her here this afternoon or tomorrow," Amos said, "introduce us to her, and explain about the honor and importance of being the next toymaker. But now . . ."

"Yes, but now . . ." Skippy the rabbit said somberly, though he had never been somber before. He glanced toward the sofa where Uncle Isaac had passed away.

Amos said, "So it's our job to go to Colleen Shannon and tell her that she must take over as toymaker."

"*Go* to her?" asked Butterscotch the dog. She padded forward from the corner. Most of her coat was soft and golden, though her tail and ears were dark brown. The white fur of her belly and chest extended over part of her face, which had a sweet and gentle look. Her paws, too, were white, as if she were wearing little boots. She looked up at Amos and frowned. "You can't be serious. How can we go to her? She's miles and miles from here."

"We've got feet, don't we?" Amos replied.

All over the workshop, Oddkins gasped in surprise upon realizing what Amos was proposing.

Thunder, like the growling of mighty machines, rolled through the sky. Lightning throbbed at the windows. A few fat drops of rain plopped against the glass, but only a few drops, then nothing more, as if the sky were hoarding the water for one great deluge.

"Go out?" Burl said from the floor below Amos's stool. He raised his plump, tightly stitched trunk as if to sniff the idea. From his expression it was clear that he did not like what he smelled. "Out of the workshop? Travel ten or twenty miles, all the way across the city to Mrs. Shannon's shop?"

His big feet thumping on the oak floor, Skippy swiftly moved in front of Burl, cocked his head in the direction of his bent ear, and said, "Well, why not, big fella? I must've heard you wish a thousand times that you were a *real* elephant and could go on treks with a herd. You keep telling us that your heart yearns for the vast plains of Africa. This would only be a little trip to the city. Nothin' to it. Why, if something gets in your way, you just tromp on it with your huge elephant feet—"

Burl looked down at his stubby little velour-skinned feet and frowned.

"—or knock 'em aside with your powerful trunk!" Skippy said with great drama, staggering backwards as if he had been hit.·

Burl wrinkled his brow and crossed his eyes in order to examine his own soft gray trunk.

Amos was pleased to have Skippy on his side. He just hoped that some other Oddkins, more responsible and less silly than the rabbit, would also side with him. Butterscotch, for one. And maybe Patch and Gibbons.

"Or," Skippy told Burl, "if you run into some troublemaker, you could gore him with those enormous and wickedly sharp tusks."

Burl's tusks were the size of the first joint of a man's thumb, covered with soft cotton, stuffed with fireproof fiber, and about as sharp as butter. But the elephant, who did indeed dream of being a real pachyderm on the African veldt, was willing to be talked into believing that he was in fact an impressive creature. He did not seem to realize that Skippy was teasing him.

"Well, I guess a little trip across the city isn't out of the question," Burl said. "I can take care of myself. Nothing out there is half as dangerous as the predators who stalk the veldt!"

"That's the spirit," Skippy said, clapping him on the back.

Thunder rumbled again. The rain was still holding back.

Butterscotch padded over to the rabbit and said, "Whether we could make the trip or not is beside the point. I mean, we can't risk being seen by adults. We must *never* be seen by anyone except the toymaker and the special children to whom we'll one day be given."

Looking down on them from the workbench stool, Amos said,

"Oh, yes, it's a frightening and dangerous idea. But Uncle Isaac is in Heaven now, watching us, and this is what he'd want us to do."

"How do you know what he'd want us to do?" asked the frog on the sofa, his deep voice echoing around the big room.

Amos frowned. "Well . . . gosh, I'm not sure *how* I know, but I know. This is what Uncle Isaac would want. Because every hour that passes without a new magic toymaker in charge of the workshop . . . well, the danger increases that a *bad* toymaker will come along."

"A bad toymaker?" said Burl.

From a shadowy corner of the workshop, old Gibbons stepped forward. "Amos is right," he said.

Gibbons was a stout, squat, long-snouted creature, the only Oddkins that was not patterned after a recognizable animal. At least none that Amos recognized. White hair streamed back from Gibbons's high forehead. He wore half-lens reading glasses on his long nose, but even without those spectacles he would have looked wise and scholarly.

His appearance fascinated all the Oddkins. More than a few of them regarded him with reverence, as children might look up to a greatly respected and beloved teacher.

Gibbons said, "Before Uncle Isaac, this workshop was run by an evil man who made magic toys that *harmed* children."

Every Oddkins in the room, except Amos, gasped in shock.

"*Harm children?*" said Butterscotch, a most gentle dog. "But that's . . . that's unthinkable!"

4.

In the subcellar, something strange was happening.

While Rex the marionette brushed the last of the dust from his tuxedo, the light from the stained-glass chandeliers grew slowly brighter. Throughout the vast chamber all signs of age and neglect began to fade. The thickly layered dust on the crates vanished as if it were water evaporating in summer heat. The cobwebs grew thin, thinner, and then disappeared.

Some power had awakened in the basement, and though this power was invisible itself, its effects could be seen.

The brittle, dry, stained wooden boxes somehow became new again. The words CHARON TOYS blazed brighter. Wherever it appeared, the company's symbol—a silhouetted gondolier poling a boat along a dark river—looked freshly painted. Within the crates, noises arose: low grumbling, soft thumping, scraping, raspy voices.

"Arise!" Rex cried. "Your time has come again!"

The eerie voices grew louder, stronger.

Some of the imprisoned toys began to pry at the lids of the crates from within, working their way out as Rex had done. Nails screeched. Wood splintered and cracked.

Rex climbed onto the top of the crate that had been his own coffin. Clenching his white-gloved wooden fists, he raised his arms above his head and shouted, "Arise! Our time has come again! Time to torment children. Time to spread darkness instead of light. A wonderful new dawn of unhappiness and fear."

From scores of wooden boxes came the bad toys of the earlier age. They had all been hiding in the subcellar, dreaming nasty dreams, ever since Mr. Bodkins had taken over the factory from the evil toymaker who had owned it during the first four and a half decades of the century. Now they were finished with dreaming and ready to bring their nasty schemes into the real world.

The boot heels of toy soldiers clicked on the cobblestone floor. Their enameled eyes were black, shiny, cold. The bayonets on their rifles had sharp, gleaming edges. The toy trucks had grilles that looked like toothy mouths; their headlights were watchful insect-like eyes. The stuffed-toy lion was not cuddly like the toys two floors above in Mr. Bodkins's workshop; this cat had a mangy, hungry look.

"The cycle begins anew!" Rex cried as the toys began to gather around on the floor, looking up at him. "Good gives way to evil. Our time has come again, and we're going to seize it!"

5.

"Harm children? Unthinkable!" Butterscotch repeated, shaking her head, dark ears flapping.

"The forces of good and evil are always present in the world," Gibbons said, putting one finger alongside his big snout, a gesture that he frequently used and by which he meant to indicate the truth and importance of what he was saying. "Sometimes evil wins," he told them somberly.

Gibbons was good at being somber.

Too good at it, Amos the bear thought. There was a danger that Gibbons would demoralize the others.

Amos quickly descended from the workbench stool to join his friends on the floor.

Gibbons was the oldest toy in the shop—and in fact he was the first creature that Mr. Bodkins had stitched together decades ago. Gibbons was not meant to be sold, and he was the only Oddkin who would never serve a special child. He was a great scholar who knew everything about the lore and history of the Oddkins. If something unexpected happened to the toymaker, it was Gibbons's sacred trust to carry his knowledge and the details of magic toymaking to the next toymaker. He took his responsibilities seriously, and his brow was permanently furrowed as a result.

"Some of those bad toys may still be hiding here," Gibbons said, scowling at them over the tops of his reading glasses.

He was dressed like a character out of a story by Dickens (Amos had read a little of Charles Dickens, so he knew about such things), like a Victorian scholar or attorney, wearing garters on his shirt sleeves, a dark suit, wide tie, and peculiar fingerless gloves. His authoritative appearance and voice held the Oddkins' attention.

"Uncle Isaac believed that below the cellar was a subcellar where the creations of the previous toymaker were stored. But he couldn't find the entrance—maybe because the way is guarded by dark magic."

Skippy the rabbit looked down at the floor. "Bad toys right under us?" His nose twitched. His tail twitched. His bent ear twitched. "*Nasty* toys?"

"Very nasty," Gibbons said.

"We can deal with them," Amos said firmly.

"Sure. If they come around here," Burl said, "I'll tromp them." He stamped one of his little elephant feet on the wooden floor for emphasis. "Squish 'em, is what I'll do. Yes, sir. Squish, squish, squish."

"And I," said Patch the cat, "will skewer them."

Patch was dressed like a cavalier in a silk shirt with wide sleeves, a green wraparound vest, a broad leather belt, and maroon trousers tucked into high boots. He wore a broad-brimmed hat with one side of the brim pinned to the crown, giving him a roguish look. The sword in his scabbard, on which he now rested one paw, was made of highly flexible rubber and could skewer no one. However, Patch believed himself to be a swordsman of great skill. And if you believe in yourself, almost anything is possible. If you believe in yourself, even a rubber sword can be a good weapon.

"I suppose I could bite them," Butterscotch said, "although I'd regret having to do such a thing even to a bad toy."

Her teeth were no sharper than Burl's tusks, but she was clearly distressed by the thought of applying even soft fangs to the enemy.

Swept up by these courageous statements, Skippy said, "And I will fight those nasties, too, if they show their faces around here."

"You?" said Patch with obvious doubt. "Just what could you do to scare them off?"

Skippy blinked. He wiggled his nose in thought. "I could thump them with one of my big flat feet," he finally declared.

Patch drew his rubber sword from its scabbard. Stroking the blade he said, "Skippy, if these black-hearted scoundrels are truly nasty, they may just cut off the foot you try to thump them with, then use it as a good-luck charm."

Skippy's ears stood straight up—even the bent one—and his eyes went wide.

Lightning flickered at the windows, and tree shadows leaped in the blood-red twilight.

Thunder clattered through the sky.

The velvet penguins began to twitter nervously. The cats stood with their backs arched, and the dogs looked around worriedly, and two of the teddy bears hugged each other for comfort. On the sofa the frog croaked unhappily and spoke of doom in a deep, rumbling voice.

Before the Oddkins could talk themselves into a state of panic, Amos took control of the situation. "We must set out for Colleen Shannon's toy shop now, without delaying another minute."

"Yes," Patch said, "before those evil toys climb up from the subcellar and try to stop us."

"Most of you will stay here," Amos said. "If worse comes to worst, you'll defend the toy factory from whatever might crawl out of the subcellar."

A small teddy bear named Ralph climbed onto the low table in front of the sofa and plucked a spoon from an empty china cup. The cup had held Uncle

Isaac's morning coffee. Ralph took half a dozen quick practice swings with the spoon, scowling with utmost seriousness while slashing at the air in front of him, as if he were wielding a deadly mace instead of a piece of silverware.

Amos was not confident that the factory could be defended by spoon-armed soldiers, but he knew that his friends were gentle by nature and could not be expected to be fierce fighters. They would just have to do the best they could.

In his most solemn, deep, and bearish voice, Amos continued: "If the Leben Toy Factory falls into *their* hands before we can reach Mrs. Shannon and convince her to take Isaac Bodkins's place, then an evil toymaker might take over. The name will be changed back to what it once was—"

"Charon Toys," Gibbons said.

"—and if that happens . . . well, it'll be too late. The factory will be lost for many years. Bad toys will be made and sold for decades, and countless children's lives will be darkened . . . ruined. . . ."

Ralph the bear swung his spoon again.

The cats hissed.

One of the dogs growled deep in his throat.

A pair of monkeys—one corduroy, one veleteen—began to gather up paper-weights, pens, pencils, figurines, and small vases that could be thrown at attackers. They piled these missiles in one corner of the room.

As the monkeys worked, Amos said, "Now, I will lead a party of Oddkins to Mrs. Shannon's toy shop. I'll need true, selfless, and courageous companions—stout of heart, swift of foot, strong of limb, quick-minded, and dependable."

"Gosh, Amos, that sounds like me," said Skippy the rabbit. The S-sounds whistled slightly between his big buck teeth.

6.

The lingering aura of Isaac Bodkins's goodness still protected the toy shop from evil. The creatures in the subcellar would not be able to ascend into the upper floors of the building and seize control until that aura had faded.

Because the Master of Darkness—the Evil One himself—spoke to Rex in a clear voice that his fellow toys could hear only as a vague whisper, the tuxedoed marionette knew that several Oddkins were about to embark upon a difficult journey to Colleen Shannon's toy shop. They would probably not survive the dangers of the night, the storm, and the city. Their chances of reaching Mrs. Shannon in time were very small, but Rex could not permit them to make the trip unchallenged.

"We must stop them," he told the malevolent crowd that gathered around him in the subcellar. "We must go after them and wipe them out. I will need assistance. Lizzie, you will come with me."

Lizzie was another marionette. She was made up like a flapper from the Roaring Twenties. She wore a sleeveless red dress with a short hemline and a long waistline, a matching hat that was tightly fitted and decorated with a small blue feather, and three strands of blue beads. Her cheeks were brightly rouged. Her hair lay across her forehead in a series of tight curls. There was a hard, cold look about her that Rex liked, a meanness in her blue eyes. She carried a black cigarette holder that contained a plastic cigarette. Like Rex, she had no strings attached to her.

Rex said, "And you, Gear, will also join us. We might have need of your strength."

Gear was a robot, the last Charon toy created before Mr. Bodkins took over the factory, a futuristic design. He was made entirely of metal and was lightly filmed with rust that steadily disappeared as the power of evil revitalized him after years of inactivity. Two small but fierce yellow lights glowed in his deep eye sockets. His lipless mouth was toothed like the jaws of a steam shovel, and his hands looked frighteningly powerful. He stepped forward, pushing through

the crowd of vicious toys, all of whom crowded forward in their eagerness to be chosen. Gear's feet clanked softly and occasionally struck a spark on the cold, stone floor.

The robot stopped in front of the crate on which Rex stood. He looked up. In a voice of ice and iron, he said, "I will tear their soft limbs apart. I will rip the stuffing out of them. I will tear them to pieces."

Something about Gear made even Rex uneasy, so he looked quickly away and pointed to Jack Weasel. "You will join us as well."

Jack Weasel was a jack-in-the-box. His red box was on wheels that boasted shiny, razor-sharp rims. His body was an accordionlike structure that rose out of the box and supported a wickedly painted clown's head. His mouth was large and red, and his teeth were yellow. The pupil of his right eye was small and green, but the pupil of his left eye was large and blood-red. He wore a ruffled clown's collar and a black derby much too small for him, although there was nothing comical about his attire. He could propel himself with two highly flexible arms that ended in four-fingered, white-gloved hands.

His wheels clicking on the stone floor, Jack rolled forward and gazed admiringly at Rex. He giggled. In a whispery voice he said, "I'll snatch one of those cuddly little Oddkins, and I'll drag him inside my box, and I'll close the lid tight, and that will be the end of him."

Jack Weasel looked perfectly mad.

He giggled again.

Rex's final choice was Stinger the bee.

This creature was made of wood with hinged metal wings and four hinged legs of wood. His yellow body was marked by black stripes. His head was yellow with large crimson eyes, and his facial features were less like those of a bee than like those of a man. When Stinger was held in a child's hand and swooped through the air, his wings would flap. He also made a buzzing sound as wind passed through a hole in his body and, in passing, turned two sets of noise-making propellers. He had red wheels, too, so he could be rolled along the floor.

Rex chose Stinger because, powered by the forces of evil, the bee could actually fly. He would be able to soar ahead of the others in search of the Oddkins and report back to Rex when he located the enemy. Besides, Stinger was a good warrior as well. His body ended in the weapon that gave him his name: a curved stinger that did not look impressive until, when needed, it telescoped out of the bee's body, becoming three times longer and much sharper than it first appeared to be.

When he heard Rex call his name, Stinger flew out of a dark corner of the subcellar. He buzzed over the heads of the other toys. He was grinning. His red eyes flashed.

"They have no chance against us," Rex said, and a low growl of agreement passed through the crowd in the subcellar.

7.

Having climbed onto the workbench again, Amos fumbled with the latch on the casement window and pulled the two halves inward. A cold gust of wind swept into the toy factory.

Nightfall was fast approaching. The fiery red western sky was turning purple. The leafless trees swayed, and the dead grass rippled like the brown surface of a muddy pool.

The other members of Amos's mission were on the bench behind him: Burl the elephant, Butterscotch the dog, Patch the cavalier cat, old Gibbons, and Skippy the rabbit. They had all said good-bye to the other Oddkins—the penguins, the gravel-throated frog, the cats and dogs and monkeys—who would remain behind to defend the factory if nasty toys did indeed climb out of the darker regions beneath the old building.

The winter-seared lawn was only a few feet below the window, and Amos urged Burl to leave quickly.

The elephant stood on the sill for a moment, hesitant. His large ears rose and fell and rose and fell as the wind got under them. "My kind were meant to rule the veldt," he told Amos. "We weren't made for jumping."

"And my kind," Amos said, "were made to eat honey and to catch fish with our paws and to hibernate in caves, but if I had to rollerskate on an airplane wing in order to accomplish what Uncle Isaac asked of me, I wouldn't hesitate."

"I'd never hibernate in a cave," Burl said, teetering on the windowsill as the wind flapped both his vest and his ears. "Mice might live in a cave. And there'd be bats, too, which are nothing but flying mice. I don't like mice. No, sir. Like all elephants, I have a healthy fear of mice. Horrid little creatures." He shivered.

Amos said, "I'm sorry to hear that . . . because there's a mouse on the workbench right behind you."

Burl squeaked in fear and jumped out of the window. He landed solidly on both stumpy feet. As lightning flickered in the darkening sky, he turned and looked up at the window, obviously surprised by his surefootedness. If he realized that he had been tricked, he was not angry; he grinned and waved his trunk at Amos.

Outside, the trees surrounding the toy factory appeared to be melting into one enormous black blot. On the lawn, shadows were lengthening. Butterscotch leaped down to the grass without hesitation, and Patch followed with the wondrous agility of his kind.

As the oldest of the six, Gibbons was the least spry. Over the decades Uncle Isaac had repaired Gibbons's stitching when necessary, but the elder creature's joints and fabric were not as flexible as they had once been. Besides, he was a scholar, bookish by nature, not created for such adventures as these.

"Can you do it?" Amos asked worriedly.

"Oh, of course," said Gibbons. He pitched his cane down onto the dead, brown grass. His long snout twitched, and he raised one eyebrow as he looked sideways at Amos. "Fortunately, my spectacles are glued to my nose." He jumped.

Skippy stepped to the window and said, "I would prefer a ladder."

"We don't have a ladder," Amos said.

"A rope will do."

"No rope."

"A parachute?" the rabbit asked.

"It's only a few feet down."

"A helium-filled balloon would be nice."

Amos planted one foot against Skippy's tail and shoved him out of the window.

The rabbit made a frantic effort to twirl his long ears as if they were the blades of a helicopter, but instead of keeping him aloft they became tangled. He hit the ground, rolled, and knocked over all of the other Oddkins who were waiting for him.

Standing on the windowsill, Amos looked down at his friends as they picked themselves up from the winter-dry grass, and he thought that they looked pathetically small and helpless. The world beyond the toy factory suddenly seemed huge, frighteningly vast. The sky was even bigger than the land beneath it: barely touched by light in the west, the blackest of blacks in the east, and full of churning storm clouds. The chilly and powerful wind chased crisp leaves across the lawn, rattled the bare branches of trees, and caused the evergreen shrubs to shiver and rustle as if they were alive. The city—and Mrs. Colleen Shannon's toy shop—seemed as far away as the moon.

Dear God, Amos thought, the world is so big, we are so small, and I'm afraid.

But then he said to himself, "Alpha and Omega. I will be the first to face up to every challenge and the last to retreat. I will be the first to forge ahead and the last to surrender to fear." He nodded and said aloud, "Okeydoke," and then he jumped.

He landed on his feet, stumbled, but did not fall. By the time he turned and looked up, a corduroy monkey named Scamp was closing the halves of the casement window. "Good luck," Scamp called to them.

"We'll need all the luck we can get," Skippy said as he peered anxiously around at the blustery night and the lowering sky.

"We'll make our own luck," said Patch, speaking with all the confidence of a heroic cavalier. His bushy tail fluttered in the wind, and the wide sleeves of his shirt billowed.

Skippy said, "Is your hat sewed to your head?"

"Sewed tight," Patch confirmed.

"Well," Skippy said, "that's *one* thing we don't have to worry about."

Amos said, "Enough talk. Let's go."

8.

Secret stone stairs led up from the subcellar to a hidden door in the wall of the first cellar. Rex, Lizzie, and Gear could climb the steps with no difficulty. Of course, Stinger flew to the top. The bee made a high-pitched buzz that reverberated between the damp walls of the stairwell, irritating Rex.

Equipped with wheels but with no legs, Jack Weasel found the climb more troublesome. However, his arms were quite powerful, so he was able to drag and pull himself from one step to the next, driven by his desire to get his hands on the Oddkins.

Neither Rex nor any of Jack's other comrades offered to help him reach the upper landing. They had been created without a single drop of mercy, without a trace of compassion, with no capacity for kindness. Although they had the same goals, and though they thought as if with a single mind, and though the same vicious desires drove them, they never considered assisting one another.

The head of the stairs was illuminated by a bare bulb in a wire cage. In that dim glow, Rex saw that perhaps a hundred spiders had ascended with them and were perched on webs overhead. They were fat, glossy black spiders with long legs, a good-bye party no doubt sent by the Master of Darkness himself.

"Little girls are afraid of spiders," Lizzie said. "One day, when I am at last sent to a toy shop and sold, I will collect the ugliest spiders I can find and hide them under my child's pillow and in her shoes."

Jack Weasel giggled with approval.

"You will have your chance with a child," Rex promised Lizzie. "Our time has come again. You'll have your chance."

Gear hooked his blunt fingers into a slot in the secret door. Straining his iron muscles, he forced the portal open wide enough to allow them to pass into the higher cellar.

Rex pointed his black cane at a ceiling light. It winked on.

He could feel the lingering aura of Bodkins's goodness; it seeped down from the factory above, where it was undoubtedly far stronger. Even though Bodkins was dead, the magic toymaker's benign influence would not fade for several hours and would be strong enough in the rooms overhead to prevent the Charon toys from seizing control. For now, they dared go no higher in the building than this cellar.

"The Oddkins have already left for Mrs. Shannon's shop," Rex said, merely telling the others what an inner voice had told him. "We've got to get out of here quickly, find those soft-bellied goody-goodies, and destroy them."

They discovered a coal bin in one corner of the cellar, climbed the pile of coal, and crawled out of the factory by way of a heavy hinged door at the top of the bin.

The lawn was windswept, and the air was cold.

Lightning stabbed through the sky. Jagged shadows leaped in the brief, bright spasm.

Thunder cracked, then rumbled overhead.

Encircling the lawn, skeletal black trees, stripped of leaves, seemed to jump forward with each flash of lightning, then retreated into darkness.

Rex laughed with delight. He loved nights like this.

9.

His name was Nick Jagg, and this was his first day of freedom in a long time. He had spent the past fifteen years in prison, for he had once committed terrible crimes. This afternoon, having served his full sentence, he had been released.

Since stopping for an early supper in a roadside diner, Jagg had been heading steadily north. He was not sure where he was going or what he would do when he got there. But he felt in his bones that he must go north. Something seemed to be *calling* him in that direction. He walked in the cold rain along the shoulder of the highway.

He wore a cheap pair of black shoes, a cheap blue suit, a white shirt, no tie, and a baggy raincoat—all of which he had received on his discharge from prison. He had a hundred dollars in his pocket. His clothes and the hundred bucks were all he owned in the world.

Tall, lean, hawk-faced, Nick Jagg looked dangerous. He could make people uncomfortable just by walking into a room. His gray eyes were almost transparent, cold as ice—and now, at night, they seemed to shine like the eyes of a wild animal.

As he walked along the highway, sometimes the rain drizzled down, and sometimes it fell with such force that it seemed that a dam had burst in the sky. Jagg's hair was plastered to his head. His shoes were soggy, and the skin of his feet had shriveled inside his wet socks. His pants were soaked by the spray from passing cars.

He was thoroughly wet, cold, and miserable, but he used his misery to fuel his hatred. Jagg hated everyone and everything. He hated the prison and every man in it. He hated the world outside the prison and everyone who lived in freedom. He hated the drivers who roared past him without offering a ride, and frequently he hurled curses at them even though they could not hear him.

Jagg even hated the drivers who stopped and picked him up. He did not curse them, but he sat in sullen silence in their cars. He would speak only a few grudging words, and he scowled at them when they tried to engage him in conversation. He made them so uneasy that none would carry him more than a few miles; therefore he spent most of the afternoon and evening walking in the rain when he could have been riding in comfort.

His only reason for living was to enjoy his hatred, to spread his evil wherever he could. He took no pleasure in books or movies or good food or music, found no joy in the beauty of the world, and never laughed. Without his hatred he would have turned to dust and blown away.

In prison, after he had served long enough to be given certain privileges, he had passed much of his time in the woodworking shop. The prisoners built simple toys that were given to various charities for distribution to needy children each Christmas.

Jagg hated all children as much as he hated all adults. He built toys with hidden flaws, wooden cars and wooden dolls that would break after only an hour or two of play. His greatest—and only—pleasure was the knowledge that the children playing with his toys would be reduced to tears when their bright new dolls and trucks and wooden-wheeled cars cracked and splintered into useless junk.

Last night, his final night in prison, Jagg had experienced a strange, vivid dream about a toy factory. The sign had said CHARON TOYS, and he had seen himself busy at a workbench, constructing a clown doll with a wicked gleam in its painted eyes.

He had recalled the dream several times today, while trudging through the rain. He was puzzled by it. No other dream had ever seemed so *real*.

Jagg was also puzzled by his own determination to keep moving northward in spite of the storm. Even with just one hundred dollars in his pocket, he could have afforded lodgings in a rooming house or a cheap motel. He could have waited until the rain passed, which would have made his journey less miserable. But he was unable to stop. He was compelled to slog on through the storm. He felt as if he were a sliver of iron being drawn northward by some enormous magnet.

My future is in the north, he thought.

But he did not know what his future might be.

The rainy highway glistened blackly.

Now and then, cars approached. Their occupants were invisible behind the glare of headlights and rain-streaked windshields. Each time he heard an engine behind him, Jagg turned and raised his thumb in the classic gesture of hitchhikers. Most of the cars sped by him. A few drivers slowed down, but when they got a closer look at Jagg, they accelerated again and disappeared into the stormy night.

A thin fog appeared like a gauzy cloak on the fields that flanked the highway. Later, there were trees bearded with fog.

Jagg trudged on.

The air grew colder.

Jagg wondered if the rain would turn to sleet or snow.

He shoved his hands deep in the pockets of his raincoat and hunched his shoulders and continued north.

2

A DARK AND
STORMY NIGHT

1.

Victor Bodkins—nephew of Isaac, the recently deceased toymaker—drove along the night-shrouded suburban lane, muttering to himself. He often muttered to himself because he did not have a wife and lived alone, and he was without close friends, so the only person to whom he could talk at any length was himself.

He was a sour man. Though he was still young, only thirty-five, he seemed seventy because his vinegary personality had made him old before his time. His face was pale, lean, pinched, and unpleasant. He always looked as if he had just bitten into a lemon. He was tall and too thin. He hunched over the wheel as he drove. When on foot, he walked with a stoop, as though a mountain was balanced on his narrow shoulders.

At the moment he was both sad and angry.

He was sad because his uncle was dead. They had never been very close, which was Victor's fault. Sweet-tempered Isaac would have delighted in a warm relationship. But Victor had neither the time nor the desire to be close to anyone. Now that Isaac was gone, however, Victor missed him. In fact, Victor was surprised at how very much he missed his Uncle Isaac.

At the same time he was angry because Isaac's life as a toymaker seemed like such a total waste. Toys were for children, not for grown men. That was Victor's view. Actually he had never much cared for toys even when he was a child. By contrast Isaac had never really grown up, which was why he was so happy to spend his life surrounded by toys. Such a waste. Such a pity.

Victor braked at a stop sign, then turned right, heading for Leben Toys, which was only about a mile away.

Lightning crackled across the dark sky.

Crisp leaves blew across the roadway, and a few scraped over the car's windshield before spinning off into the darkness.

He would have preferred to be snug at home on a night like this. Besides, he had business magazines to read, bank accounts to balance, potential investments to explore and evaluate. He usually worked fourteen hours a day, seven days a week, and he was uneasy when he was not working.

Perhaps Victor would have approved if Isaac had owned a *real* toy factory, a huge operation with a thousand machines stamping out dolls and miniature trucks and a hundred other products at the rate of one every two seconds. There was money in big-time toy manufacturing, and Victor thoroughly approved of money. But Isaac had earned very little from his toys, barely enough to keep himself fed and clothed. He made toys for the pure love of it. Such a waste. Such a pity.

Now the property of Leben Toys belonged to Victor, for he and Isaac were the last living members of their family, and Victor was determined to make the business finally pay off. First he would inventory the stock and all of Isaac's tools—and sell everything. The rambling old house of many gables, in which Isaac had lived and worked, would have to be demolished. It was no doubt a creaking, drafty place that needed new wiring and plumbing, and it must cost a fortune to heat those high-ceiling rooms.

Eventually the four surrounding acres could be subdivided, and a dozen suburban homes could be erected at a fine profit. He had often tried to convince Isaac to use the property for this purpose, but Isaac had a sentimental attachment to the toy factory and had not known what was best for him.

Victor, on the other hand, was prepared to sell to the highest bidder.

2.

A stone footbridge, fitted with domed lamps at both ends, crossed the swift-flowing stream that ran in front of Leben Toys. Amos led the Oddkins across the bridge while Gibbons told them the history of the structure.

"Erected in the summer of 1786, one year after the house was built," he said, raising his reedy voice to compete with the moaning wind. "The great Thomas

Jefferson walked across this bridge on two different occasions. Years later, Abraham Lincoln came by to purchase a few toys for the children of some friends. Abe was so taken with the natural beauty hereabouts that he spent the day fishing from this little bridge. He didn't catch anything, but he said it wasn't the catching that interested him anyway; it was the fishing itself that he enjoyed."

Gibbons was interrupted by the arrival of a big dog.

A very big dog.

Big and mean.

As Amos led the Oddkins to the end of the footbridge, a black and tan mongrel appeared on the stone footpath in front of them. It was half again as tall as Amos and must have weighed three times as much as all six of the Oddkins put together. It wore a heavy collar from which dangled a short length of broken chain. For a moment the dog looked startled. Then its eyes narrowed, and it growled deep in its throat.

The Oddkins froze.

The hulking mongrel peeled its pebbled black lips back in a snarl, revealing yellow teeth. Sharp teeth. *Huge* teeth.

Amos desperately thought, *Uncle Isaac, if you wanted me to be the leader, why did you make me so small? Why didn't you make me six feet tall?*

The dog lowered its head, flattened its ears against its squarish skull, and looked from one Oddkin to another.

"We're finished," Skippy said miserably.

"I'll deal with this monster," Patch said, bravely drawing his rubber sword.

"We'll be torn to pieces," Skippy said.

"Not when the beast realizes he's up against an elephant," Burl said proudly. "He hasn't noticed me yet, but when he sees me, he'll put his tail between his legs and run for his life." Burl stamped one small velour foot as if he expected the stone bridge to shake and the night to echo with the impact.

"Torn to *little* pieces," Skippy said.

Lightning flashed, and thunder exploded in the heavens, but the brute was not fazed by the oncoming storm. It advanced one step, then another, growling continuously. Saliva drooled from one corner of its mouth.

"Stay calm," Amos told his friends while frantically searching his mind for a plan to defend them from the mongrel.

"Little *tiny* pieces," Skippy said.

"Are you afraid, rabbit?" Patch demanded.

"Me?" Skippy said, offended. "I've got a heritage of courage, you know. Was old Br'er Rabbit ever afraid? Was Bugs Bunny ever afraid?" To prove himself, Skippy stepped forward, straight toward the dog, almost into its long shadow. "Hey, you ugly brute!"

The dog faced Skippy. Lightning flashed again, and for an instant the hound's eyes turned silver.

"You look as dumb as a post," Skippy said. "Too dumb to deal with the likes of us. You'd better scoot out of here before we tie your tail in knots. Fact is, I'll bet the closest you ever came to a brainstorm was a light drizzle."

The dog glared.

"Stop it, Skippy," Amos said.

But Skippy, who had dreams of being a stage comedian, was on a roll and reluctant to stop. "In a battle of wits," he told the mongrel, "you'd be unarmed."

The dog stared.

"Ah, but brains aren't everything. In fact, in your case, they're nothing at all."

The dog blinked.

"Skippy . . ." Amos warned.

But the rabbit pointed at the dog and said, "I hear you're so dumb that when you wanted to raise a litter of puppies you planted a piece of dogwood."

The foul-tempered beast lowered its head farther and barked ferociously at Skippy.

"*Eep!*" the rabbit said, and he backed up so fast that he fell over Burl.

Getting to his feet and brushing off his vest, Burl shouted at the mongrel: "I'm an elephant, you know!"

"Ummm," Gibbons said, putting one finger aside his long snout, "perhaps we'd be well advised to retreat to the house, find a bit of food, and make a peace offering to this creature."

"He'll pounce on us before we get halfway back," Patch said. "Maybe I should whap him on the nose with the flat side of my sword, put a little fear into the varlet."

Amos was angry with himself for his failure to think of a way to scare off the dog. He poised for a headlong rush at the animal, hoping to startle it into flight.

But suddenly Butterscotch trotted past Amos and addressed the mongrel: "Shame on you. You're no credit to our species."

The black and tan dog snarled again, and foamy spittle flew from his lips.

Butterscotch said, "A dog is man's best friend. A dog should be noble, true, affectionate, and kind. Did your mother teach you no manners? If you were a pup of mine, you'd have learned a thing or two about polite behavior. Shame. Oh my, yes, shame on you."

The beast stopped snarling, cocked his head, and looked puzzled.

"Just imagine what your poor mother would think if she could see you now," Butterscotch said. "She would be embarrassed for you and ashamed for having failed to raise a good dog."

At first Amos could not understand what trick Butterscotch was up to, but after a while he realized that she was not up to any trick at all; she was being sincere. She was genuinely embarrassed that a *dog* should behave as he did. In her soft, gentle voice could be heard sadness, dismay, and a scolding note. "A dog that is not a credit to his mother is a sad, wretched thing indeed. Your mother gave you life, after all. Mothers should be respected and cherished. Every act of your life should honor your mother instead of shaming her.''

Butterscotch's deeply felt emotion and stern disapproval seemed to be getting through to the vicious mongrel. The big dog was no longer growling. He licked his lips and blinked and looked sheepish.

Trotting off the end of the bridge and onto the stone footpath, Butterscotch brazenly circled the beast, looking him up and down as if she were a judge and as if this real dog were a low-life scoundrel about to be sentenced to prison. The mongrel turned in place, watching Butterscotch as she boldly circled him.

''Broke your chain, I see,'' said Butterscotch. ''Ran away from home. You haven't given a thought to the worry you're causing your master. Oh, no, not a thought for such things in the selfish head of a bad dog like you. Off on your own adventures, thinking only of yourself, eager to chase poor frightened cats and terrorize a few stuffed animals not even half your size. Your poor mother. Oh, dear me, your poor, poor mother. I feel so sorry for her.''

The mongrel made a curious whimpering sound.

Amos and the other Oddkins watched Butterscotch with astonishment and awe.

Completing a full circle of the beast, Butterscotch said, "Well, you might be able to tear us all to shreds. But that doesn't make you a big shot. That just makes you a bully, a discredit to your mother and your litter, a discredit to the entire noble race of dogs."

The mongrel whined and hung his head.

"Ashamed? I should think so. If you have any hope of redeeming yourself and one day bringing credit to your loving mother, I'd advise you to put your tail between your legs right now, slink home, lick the hand of your master, and do what you're told from now on. In time there might even be a place in the pastures of Heaven for you, though right now I think you're destined to spend eternity running on sore and bleeding feet through a much hotter place than Heaven."

The mongrel turned from them. With his belly nearly dragging on the ground, he crept away. Twice he looked back, and twice Butterscotch gently but scornfully told him to get along. In twenty steps he disappeared into the darkness under the leafless, wind-rattled trees.

Butterscotch returned to her friends and said, "Please forgive him for his uncouth behavior. Perhaps he was mistreated by a mean master or tormented by ill-mannered children. Of course, no matter what he might have endured, there's absolutely no excuse for his rudeness."

"You're amazing," Amos told her.

"I doff my hat to you, brave lady," Patch said gallantly. But of course his cavalier's hat was sewn to his head, so he nearly pulled himself off his feet and nearly threw himself to the ground when he attempted that chivalrous gesture.

Butterscotch blinked. "Whatever are you talking about?"

Burl stepped forward, putting his stumpy hands on his broad hips. "I can tell you right now that I'd be very proud if you'd been *my* mother."

"If she'd been your mother," Skippy said, "you'd be a dog instead of an elephant."

"To be *her* pup," Burl said, "I suppose I could give up my trunk and my dreams of the veldt."

"Genetics is an interesting subject," Gibbons said, leaning with both hands on his cane. "If Butterscotch were Burl's mother, perhaps he'd be not an ordinary pup but a dogephant. Or an elephound."

"We've got a mission," Amos reminded them. "And we've no time to waste."

Suddenly the wind picked up, shrieking in the trees.

"Follow me," Amos said, hurrying off the footbridge, along the stone path, toward the dirt lane that led down to the paved highway.

3.

A moment after climbing from the cellar and crawling into the night through the exterior door of the coal bin, Rex heard a dog barking. As the other Charon toys struggled out of the hole behind him, Rex said, "I'll wager it's cornered our little friends. If we can find the dog, we'll find our prey as well."

The barking stopped before they could get a fix on it. But the howling wind sounded like a hound at times, leading them repeatedly in the wrong direction.

"Stinger!" Rex said at last. "Fly high and find the Oddkins, then report back to me here."

The bee said, "Yes, yes, yessss, I will do it, yesssss," in a shrill little voice that sounded not unlike the high-pitched whine of a dentist's drill. He swooped up into the windy night with a furious thrumming of metal wings.

4.

Victor Bodkins turned off the highway onto the dirt lane that led to the toy factory. A few dead leaves, harried by the wind, tumbled across the road, and dry grass shivered at the verge. From both sides, huge oaks, stripped of all foliage, reached their barren limbs toward one another, forming a tunnel of sorts.

Isaac's house was still out of sight. However, having drawn this near to the place, Victor felt a sudden deepening of his sadness. In no hurry to reach the house, he slowed the car, for the task of sorting through Isaac's belongings would be depressing.

"If only you had grown up," Victor said, as if his uncle could hear him. "If only you'd faced the fact that there's no magic in life, no wonder. . . . If only you'd given up your childish belief in miracles and in the goodness of other people. . . . If only you'd learned that life is hard and cruel, maybe we wouldn't have been such strangers to each other. Perhaps we could have been closer, more like an uncle and a nephew ought to be. Ah, Isaac, you were such a hopeless dreamer."

He drove around a bend and saw six small creatures crossing the lane. For an instant he thought they were ordinary animals, a pack of cats or squirrels or raccoons, but then he blinked and got a better look at them. They were stuffed animals, toys.

Toys!

Victor saw a teddy bear in a blue sweater, a dog, a rabbit in a vest. He saw a cat in a cavalier's costume. An elephant wearing pants held up by suspenders. There was another creature he could not quite identify.

The toys froze, startled by his appearance. The roar of the pre-storm wind had evidently masked the sound of his car.

Victor tramped on the brakes and stared through the windshield in disbelief.

The toys stared back at him.

Isaac's toys. No doubt of that.

Victor remembered the teddy bear from his last visit. And the unnameable thing, dressed like a character out of Dickens, had been in Isaac's workshop for

as long as Victor could remember. Isaac had called them Oddkins.

The elephant turned to the teddy bear and appeared to speak to him. The other toys also turned to the bear as if seeking guidance.

I've lost my mind, Victor thought.

The cat's tail plumed in the wind.

The elephant's ears lifted tentatively like a pair of kites testing the air currents.

The bear shook his head and motioned with one arm for the other toys to follow him. They hurried across the road, into the darkness under the trees.

5.

Thunder boomed, and the churning masses of black clouds were briefly revealed in a zigzagging bolt of lightning. The storm would break at any moment.

Stinger plummeted down from the night sky, halted in midair, and hovered in front of Rex. "Thissss way, thissss way, I've found them, thissss way."

Like a pack of hungry, frenzied rats, the Charon toys scurried across the dead lawn, over the footbridge, along a stone path.

They encountered a large black and tan dog trailing a length of broken chain. It slunk out of some shrubbery, eyed them curiously, then seemed to want to be friends. It whined, wagged its tail, and appeared to be in need of approval and affection.

"Out of our way!" Rex commanded.

The dog did not seem to understand. It whimpered and wagged its tail more energetically than ever.

The plastic cigarette in Lizzie's holder suddenly lit, although no match had been touched to it. She cast a sly sideways look at Rex. He nodded. Lizzie smiled and pushed the hot end of the cigarette against one of the dog's paws.

The mutt yipped in surprise and pain.

Gear grabbed one of its floppy ears and yanked hard.

Rolling its eyes at the robot, the dog leaped onto its hind feet. Gear was lifted off the ground, but he held fast.

Jack Weasel giggled hysterically.

Rex stepped in front of the terrified dog as it dropped onto all fours and finally threw Gear off. The marionette pressed a button on his sleek black cane, and the knife popped into sight. "Out of our way, you stinking mongrel!"

At the same moment Stinger swooped down with his needle-sharp lance extended to three times it normal length. He stung the dog on the right flank.

Howling, the mutt fled.

"Thissss way, thissss way." Buzzing under the low-hanging branches, Stinger led his comrades along a narrow dirt path through a short stretch of woods. Rex, Lizzie, and Gear had no trouble with the wild terrain, but Jack Weasel had some difficulty pulling himself along the rutted track.

They came to the edge of a dirt lane, where they hid behind thick weeds. Rex saw no sign of the Oddkins, but a car was stopped nearby, and a tall, thin man was climbing out of it.

6.

With his rubber sword in his right hand, Patch was the last in the procession of Oddkins as they made their way through another arm of the woods, onto a narrow meadow, and down the open grassy slope toward the main highway. He repeatedly looked behind them, guarding the rear, and he almost wished that some evil toy would appear so they could engage in a satisfying fencing match.

Though the others dreaded the journey to the city, Patch rather looked forward to it. He liked action and excitement. He was a scaler of walls and leaper of gulfs, a swordsman without superior. Isaac Bodkins, his creator, had given Patch a taste for adventure, and now Patch was looking forward to this night's encounters with danger.

However, he was *not* looking forward to getting his clothes dirty. He had never imagined that adventuring could be such a filthy affair. Already, his boots were dusty and scuffed. He took some comfort from the fact that, as a cat, his night vision was better than that of his friends, so they could not see the mournful condition of his boots as clearly as he could. But somehow he had also acquired a spot of dirt on the left sleeve of his cream-colored shirt. And bits of grass and dead leaves clung to his trousers. He longed for a chance to stop and groom himself, but Amos led them through the woods and down the open sloping meadow without pause.

They were still more than fifty yards from the highway when the sky exploded with a series of lightning blasts, and thunder shook the night, and the rain came at last, abruptly and in torrents. The hard downpour flattened the meadow grass. The drumming noise was almost deafening. In seconds Patch's clothes were soaked. With horror he realized that the dry earth would quickly turn to mud and that his dashing costume would become increasingly soiled as the long night wore on.

Patch the cat was not afraid of either known dangers or the unknown. Evil toys, wild dogs, and other villains did not worry him in the least. But to be seen in wet and filthy clothes, with a soggy hat and mud caked on his boots—*that* was frightening.

7.

Victor Bodkins had taken a flashlight from the glove compartment of his car and had ventured into the gloomy woods to search for the six stuffed animals that had crossed the road in his headlight beams. Here and there he found signs that might have indicated that the small creatures had passed this way—trampled grass, broken weeds, curious marks in the soft earth—but he could not get a glimpse of the toys themselves.

"You're dreaming," he told himself as he poked among the trees. "Pinch yourself and wake up."

So he pinched himself.

But he did not wake up.

He pinched himself again, harder than before.

"Ouch," he said.

He still did not wake up.

He pinched himself again: "Ouch!"

And yet again: "Ouch!"

He was a stubborn man.

When rain began to fall, the leafless trees did not provide much of an umbrella, and he was soon soaked.

Shivering, sneezing, feeling foolish, he headed back toward the lane, where the car waited with its engine running and lights blazing. As he stepped onto the dirt roadway, he thought he saw movement out of the corner of his eye, something scurrying into the narrow drainage channel twenty feet away. He rushed to that place, but his light revealed only a trickle of muddy water.

He stepped across the ditch into the weeds along the perimeter of the woods. As he moved, he swept the beam of the flashlight back and forth—and suddenly he saw something even stranger than the six stuffed animals. It was a fourteen-inch-tall toy robot with evil yellow eyes aglow with menace and a nasty mouth cracked open in a wicked, jagged smile. It was standing half-concealed by a clump of dead, dry, drooping milkweed, looking up defiantly at Victor.

He stooped and leaned forward to pick up the robot, but it moved more swiftly than he would have thought possible, dashing under his arm. Beaded with rain, its metal skin glinted in the flashlight beam. The creature went straight to his feet, where it hammered both metal fists on the toe of his left shoe. He never would have imagined that a toy could possess such strength; the blows were hard, painful.

As Victor stumbled backward in surprise, he felt something grab hold of the right leg of his trousers. When he looked down he saw a tuxedoed marionette—with top hat but minus control strings—grinning ferociously at him.

I've gone mad, he thought. *Stark, raving mad.*

The marionette pulled hard on the trousers. Because Victor was already off balance, he almost fell.

Another marionette, a vile looking little woman in a flapper's costume from the 1920s, seized the other leg of his pants and pulled hard in that direction.

Victor swatted at the male marionette, then at the female, trying to use his flashlight as a club. He missed both of them.

The robot pounded on Victor's toes again, and a new burst of thunder was timed to the toy's blows, so it seemed as if the thing's fists had made that colossal sound.

Victor kicked out, knocking the small, metal man aside.

Suddenly a grotesque, clown-faced jack-in-the-box rolled out of the weeds, propelling himself with gloved hands. He was giggling shrilly, hysterically. ''Bring him down!'' the jack-in-the-box cried. ''Bring him down to our level!''

Streaking out of the rainswept darkness, a toy bee the size of a beer can swooped past Victor's face, startling him. In the backsplash of his own flashlight, he saw a stinger as big as a switchblade knife. A moment later, when he realized that the bee was dive-bombing him, he threw himself to the ground to avoid being stabbed.

He felt the bee bullet by his head, missing his face by only an inch or two. The instant he hit the ground, he began to thrash with both arms and legs to keep the hostile toys away.

He heard one of the impossible little creatures say, "Leave him. Come on! The Oddkins will be heading down to the highway. We've got to stop them."

Victor continued thrashing until he was exhausted. When at last he lay limp on the wet ground, he still half-expected to be attacked. But the robot, the marionettes, the jack-in-the-box, and the bee were gone. He was alone in the stormy night.

Heart hammering, he got to his feet. He was shaky.

He picked up his flashlight, swept the beam around him.

Nothing.

He looked at the woods into which the toys had evidently gone, and he considered pursuing them. Then he turned and ran back to his car, fearing for both his life and his sanity.

In the car he locked the doors.

He sat there in the middle of the muddy lane, staring through the rain-washed windshield at the portion of the roadway and woods that were revealed in his headlamps. He could not stop shaking.

He pinched himself.

"Ouch!"

Again.

"Ouch!"

He could not make sense of these events. They did not compute. He was a man of reason, a man of logic, a man who worked with numbers and trusted numbers. He *loved* numbers. There were no surprises in numbers, no magic, no mystery. He prefered life without magic and mystery, and he did not know how he would cope if he discovered that the world was actually more as Isaac had always seen it and less like the ordered and logical place that Victor had believed it to be.

"Ouch!"

One more pinch.

"Ouch!"

Just one more.

"Ouch!"

8.

Following Amos, Burl and the other Oddkins safely reached a truckstop along the highway. An orange and purple neon sign—HARLEY'S PLACE, GAS AND EATS, TRUCKERS WELCOME—blazed on the roof of the long, single-story building. Those brilliant neon colors were reflected in the wet and puddled pavement; they shimmered and rippled, so it almost seemed as if a fire burned in the blacktop without consuming it.

Harley's Place was busy out front, where trucks and a few cars were pulled up at the clusters of gasoline pumps. Out there, the big plate-glass windows of the restaurant provided a view of the highway and the rainy night.

But to the side of the building, where forty or fifty enormous trucks were parked in orderly rows, there was little activity. Once in a while a new truck arrived, and the driver dashed from his rig, through the wet night, into Harley's Place. Less often a driver came out of the restaurant, hurried to his truck, and roared back onto the highway. For the most part, however, the lot was deserted and silent but for the hiss and patter of falling rain.

Burl and the other Oddkins followed Amos around the deepest puddles, through the reflected fire of orange and purple neon, into the purple-black shadows under one of the gigantic vehicles. They huddled out of the wind and rain, thoroughly soaked and miserable.

That is, most of them were miserable, but Burl did not mind the storm at all because somewhere he had gotten the idea that elephants were supposed to enjoy water. In Africa elephants liked to laze in rivers and wallow for hours in cool ponds. Therefore striving to be the perfect little elephant, Burl had sometimes walked with his face turned up to the driving rain, relishing the feel of the thousands of droplets snapping against his velour face. While the others had gone around all the big puddles, Burl had sloshed straight through them, ignoring the peculiar looks from his fellow Oddkins, making quiet snorting sounds of pleasure.

Now, Amos and Butterscotch and Gibbons and Skippy and Patch huddled together beneath the truck, dejected. Forlornly, they looked out at the rain bouncing off the parking lot, where the big puddles grew even bigger.

Burl moved among them, giving them a pep talk. "Not so bad, the rain. We elephants love it. Very good for the skin. Keeps the trunk lubricated and limber."

"I don't *have* a trunk," Skippy said sourly.

"Well," Burl said, "I'm sorry about that. Everyone ought to have a trunk."

"I didn't say I wanted a trunk."

"Well, of course, you want a trunk. Who doesn't? A trunk is a marvelous and beautiful thing. Maybe if you say your prayers every night, without fail, then God might give you a trunk of your own some day."

Skippy looked at him strangely.

Embarrassed for his trunkless friend, Burl said, "But you have wonderfully big ears, differently shaped than mine but big in their own way . . . and rain is good for the ears, too."

"Where do you get all these silly ideas?" Skippy asked.

"They're not silly, not at all. Rain *is* good for you."

"Okay, so what *genius* told you all this about the healthfulness of rain?"

"No one had to tell me," Burl said. "I simply know it. You see, we elephants are very in tune with nature. Bears like Amos spend half their lives in hibernation, so they're not as much *aware* of nature as we elephants are. Cats like Patch and dogs like Butterscotch are domesticated animals, out of touch with nature. Rabbits live in their warrens underground, which perhaps puts them in tune with the earth but not with the rain. Ah, rain! Wonderful rain! You should all be enjoying it."

"Look what it's done to my clothes," Patch said unhappily. "I'm soaked, rumpled, a thorough mess."

"Your clothes will dry out," Burl assured him.

"Look at the mud on my boots!" Patch said, his voice thick with disgust.

"Mud will wash off," Burl said.

"My hat brim is going to droop," Patch said.

"It'll only make you more dashing, more mysterious."

Patch looked hopeful. "You really think so?"

"Nothing like a down-turned hat brim to lend an air of mystery to a cat such as yourself," Burl assured him.

Patch sighed. "I never thought adventuring would be so messy."

"At least your joints aren't arthritic like mine," Gibbons said.

Only Amos and Butterscotch did not complain, though they looked as weary and uncomfortable as everyone else.

Burl said, "Well, I've a mind to walk out there and roll around in one of those huge puddles, have a really good wallow."

"You'll do nothing of the sort," Amos said, startling Burl. "We already let ourselves be seen by Victor Bodkins. That's something we should *never* have done— let an adult get a glimpse of us."

"It wasn't our fault," Butterscotch said. "The noise of the storm prevented us from hearing the car coming."

"I should have been more careful," Amos said. "I'm the leader, after all. It's part of my job to anticipate trouble and avoid it. I'm not doing a very good job of leading, I'm afraid."

"We've gotten this far all right," Butterscotch said.

"This isn't even one percent of the way," Amos said.

"You'll get us through," Butterscotch assured him. "Now what do you propose we do next?"

Amos thought for a moment.

Rain drizzled on all sides of the truck. The air stank of grease and oil from the drive shaft and gears and other machinery above the Oddkins' heads.

Out on the highway an air horn bleated.

Finally, in a brighter tone of voice, Amos said, "I'm reminded of an appropriate bit of verse by Rupert Toon—"

Burl groaned, as did all the other Oddkins, even Butterscotch.

"Not Rupert Toon," Patch said.

"Tie my ears together and hang me from a hook," Skippy said, "but please don't make me listen to Rupert Toon poetry."

"I'll have you know," Amos said, "that Mr. Rupert Toon is a great poet. I've read books of poetry in Uncle Isaac's library, so I know about these things. One day I intend to write poetry of my own, and I only hope I can write half as well as Rupert Toon."

Burl said, "You give us that same speech every time, but somehow it doesn't make me appreciate Toon any more."

"You may be a good elephant, very knowledgeable about the African veldt and the benefits of rainwater," Amos said, "but you've got no appreciation for the finer things in life."

"Get it over with," Skippy said. "Recite this bit of Toonian slop and be done with it."

Another truck pulled into the lot and parked, and they waited for the roar of its engine to cut off.

Then Amos stood very straight, puffed out his chest, and lovingly recited the verse:

> When your footsies have been overused,
> walked on, run on, and totally abused,
> when you're sore from toesies to heels,
> better trade in your shoes for wheels.

"*'Footsies'?*" Skippy said. "How can Toon be a great poet when he uses words like 'footsies'?"

"A poet has the freedom to coin his own words when he needs to," Amos explained.

A fierce gust of wind swept across the parking lot, shrieking like a banshee.

Raising his voice to compete with the storm, Gibbons said, "And you say this Toon has won the Nobel Prize for Literature?"

"Well," Amos said, "I'm not sure if it was the Nobel—but it was some big prize."

"Not the Nobel," Skippy said. "The Dumbbell Prize."

Patch said, "Toon's poems sound the way my clothes look. I'm completely a mess. How embarrassing."

As the wind subsided again, as the shrieking faded into a low moan, Burl said, "All right, all right, so how does this Toon poem apply to our current situation?"

"It's obvious," Amos said. "It's a long way into the city, and already we're tired—so we need wheels. We'll hitch a ride in the back of one of these big trucks."

"But how will we know if the one we choose is headed toward the city or away from it?" Gibbons inquired.

"Uncle Isaac's in Heaven, watching over us," Amos said. "He won't let us choose the wrong truck."

9.

Rex led his gang of evil toys through a hole in a chain link fence and onto the pavement at the edge of the parking lot.

"They're here somewhere," he said, surveying the parked trucks, which looked like rows of prehistoric beasts slumbering in the night.

"Yes," Lizzie said, "they're here, all right. You can feel their goodness in the air."

"Disgusting, isn't it?" Jack Weasel said.

Gear worked his metal jaws, making grinding noises, and repeatedly flexed his metal hands. Stinger buzzed in circles above their heads.

"Let's go get them," Rex said. "Let's tear them limb from limb and make pillow stuffing out of them."

10.

Hours of walking brought Nick Jagg into a small town more than a hundred miles south of the city. It was an old burg, most of it dating back to the 1700s. All the buildings were brick and stone.

Jagg knew that most people would think the village was unusually pretty, but he hated it. He hated old, historic buildings partly because history bored him but mostly because you were *supposed* to like these aged structures, and Nick Jagg would never like anything that anyone told him he was supposed to like.

Of course, he hated new buildings, too, which were mostly cold-looking with lots of sharp angles. The prison in which he had spent the last half of his fifteen-year term had been a modern, clean place designed with efficiency in mind, so he hated anyplace that reminded him of that penitentiary.

He was tired and wet to the skin. His cheap shoes, issued by the prison, were soaked and slowly beginning to come apart at the seams. Rain found its way under the collar of his coat, so his suit jacket and shirt were damp. He felt dirty, clammy, and exhausted. He should have found a room for the night, but something drew him toward the center of the sleepy hamlet.

Four streets met at a town circle that had a small park in the center. Besides an area of brown grass and winter-barren flower beds, the park boasted two towering maple trees and a large, three-bowled marble fountain. The fountain was turned off, but the bowls were overflowing with rainwater.

On the other side of the street, all the way around the circle, were shops: antique stores, an ice-cream parlor, a barbershop and a beauty parlor, a few dress shops, a bookstore. They were all closed and dark except for the lights in their display windows.

There was also a small bus station, and when Jagg saw it he knew that the station was the place that had drawn him to the town circle. Feeling strange, almost as if he were hypnotized, he walked to the front door of the terminal and stepped inside, into the harsh fluorescent glare.

A single clerk was sitting at the far end of the room behind a counter, reading a paperback book. A radio was playing music from the 1940s.

It felt good to be in a warm, dry place.

Something on the floor glinted and caught Jagg's attention. He looked down and saw a brass key on the green tiles. He stooped, plucked it off the tiles, and noticed a number on it.

The station clerk had not looked up from his book.

Feeling very strange indeed, still moving as if he were just a marionette being controlled by a puppetmaster, Jagg walked past a group of wooden benches to a row of luggage lockers. He found the locker with the same number as the key and opened it. Inside was a single suitcase. He had never seen this piece of luggage before, but his initials were on it: NJ.

He carried the suitcase into the men's room and opened it on the counter beside the sink. It was packed full of one-hundred-dollar bills. A few thousand of them.

"What's this?" Jagg said, finally shocked out of his trance.

A soft but deep voice said, "It's money to buy the toy factory."

Startled, Jagg turned and looked around.

He was still alone in the brightly lighted men's room. No one had entered behind him.

"Look in the mirror, Jagg."

He whirled toward the sink. Where he should have seen his own reflection in the age-spotted mirror, he saw instead a shadowy face that was not entirely human.

The awful eyes were sunken and glowed a smoky, sullen red. The mouth was too large for a human mouth . . . and seemed to be full of exceedingly sharp teeth.

"The toy factory in your dream last night," said the beast in the mirror. "Your destiny is to own it."

"Why?"

"You will be the new toymaker."

Jagg did not have to ask the name of the creature to whom he spoke. In his heart he knew the beast's identity. It was the Dark One, the Master of Evil. Though Jagg had never actually seen the Devil before, he had always been close to him.

"Toymaker?" Jagg said. "But I hate toys. I hate children."

"Of course, you do," said the hideous thing in the mirror. It grinned at him. "That's why it's your destiny. Times are changing. Evil is on the rise. The toy factory and many other things will be falling into my hands in the days to come. You will build toys that will do great harm to the children who own them, toys that will bring pain and misery and enormous sadness to everyone they touch. You must get to the city tonight, without delay. You will find a man named Victor Bodkins, and you will offer him cash for the factory. He can't resist cash. He loves cash."

The face faded from the mirror, and in a while Jagg could see his own face staring back at him, pale and wide-eyed.

He would be a toymaker with his own factory. Though he did not yet understand how his toys would harm children, he knew that this was indeed his destiny.

Heart hammering, excited, as close to happiness as he had ever been, Nick Jagg closed the suitcase, carried it into the waiting room, went to the counter, and bought a ticket to the city on the next bus out.

3
BIG CITY,
SMALL VISITORS

1.

The Oddkins will be heading down to the highway. We've got to stop them. Those had been the words of the tuxedo-clad marionette when he had urged the robot, the bee, and the other toys to leave Victor Bodkins and pursue the stuffed toys instead. Hoping to catch sight of one of the impossible creatures again, Victor drove back to the main highway and turned north.

Hunching over the steering wheel, he eased the car slowly along the gravel shoulder, peering intently into the rain-lashed gloom at the edge of the dark woods. He was seeking a tiny flicker of the robot's glowing yellow eyes or the darting flight of the soda-can-size bee or the hurried movement of the stuffed toys that he had first seen crossing the lane in his headlights.

He realized that these creatures were quite small and that the forest was large. He knew there was little chance that he would get another look at the toys. But he could not give up easily. He had been given a glimpse of something wondrous, something magical. Suddenly his entire orderly, disciplined way of life was trembling under him as if it were a rickety bamboo platform. He *had* to know what they were, where they came from—and what connection they had with his uncle.

In time he came to a roadside restaurant and service station. The enormous orange and purple neon sign on the roof—HARLEY'S PLACE, EATS AND GAS, TRUCKERS WELCOME—seemed bigger than the building under it. The falling rain was tinted by the neon and looked like millions of strands of gaudy tinsel.

Victor pulled into the parking lot, intending to pause there for a few minutes to think. As he entered, he passed two trucks that were heading out to the highway. The first was an olive-green United States Army transport, the cargo bed of which was enclosed with wood and canvas. One canvas flap at the rear was loose and billowing in the wind. The second truck had a long, open bed that was piled high with eight-foot lengths of large, steel pipes held in place by chains and wooden wedges.

As the second truck slowly rumbled past only two feet to the left of Victor's car, he was startled to see the male marionette perched on the cargo. It was standing on a wooden wedge, gripping a chain with one small hand and the rim of a steel pipe with the other. It was leaning out to peer forward past the cab of its own truck toward the back of the army transport. Rain drizzled off the brim of the wicked-looking creature's top hat.

The truck continued to roll by, and the marionette slid out of sight. Then Victor saw the toy robot. It was half in and half out of one of the stacked pipes. It turned its evil, glowing yellow eyes on Victor as they passed each other. They were separated only by the car window, a couple of feet of open air, and thin curtains of neon-colored rain. The robot's arm drew back and snapped forward in a throwing motion. A small object—maybe a pebble, perhaps a scrap of wood or metal—struck the side window of Victor's car, directly in front of his face. He flinched. The glass did not crack.

Behind Victor the truck pulled out onto the rainy highway, carrying the robot and marionette and other toys away into the storm.

Victor pinched himself.

"Ouch!"

Then he frantically turned the car around.

The chase had begun.

2.

After much struggle Amos and Patch finally secured the loose flap of canvas at the back of the army truck. Having sealed out the wind and rain, they joined the other Oddkins who were huddled together in the gloom.

The truck's cargo space was only three-quarters full. It was carrying bales of olive-green wool army blankets. The only light was a grayish glow that came through a small, wire-covered window between the rear area and the cab.

The Oddkins had settled into a shallow, empty space among the bales of blankets, where they could just barely see one another in the faint light. They could not be seen by the driver or his partner if either man happened to look back through the narrow window.

Amos was saddened by his friends' wet and miserable appearance. But he was also beginning to feel better about his leadership, for he had gotten them onto a truck headed for the city. He was doing what his Uncle Isaac had trusted him to do. A low flame of pride had begun to burn in him.

They spoke quietly even though the rumble of the engine, the howl of the wind, and the roar of the rain were sufficiently loud to ensure that they were not overheard. They remembered how they accidentally had let themselves be seen by Uncle Isaac's nephew, Victor, and they were determined not to reveal their presence to another adult—except, of course, to Mrs. Colleen Shannon at her toy shop.

At first, as if they were experienced adventurers enjoying the memory of a major triumph, they talked about their flight from the toy factory and their frightening encounter with the mongrel dog on the footbridge.

"I taught that beast the meaning of fear," Skippy said. "Did you see the way he flinched from my witty insults?"

Amos knew Skippy was not sticking to the facts. But he thought it might do their morale some good if they allowed themselves to exaggerate the courage they had shown.

Skippy said, "If you make jokes at a bully's expense and make him seem foolish, you reduce his power over you."

"It might be true that being able to laugh at a bully makes him less frightening," said Burl, nodding and waving his trunk. "But you didn't scare that mongrel, Skippy."

"Sure I did," the rabbit said. "He was shivering and whimpering by the time I was finished with him."

"No, dear rabbit, you misremember," Burl said kindly.

"Whimpering and whining."

"No, your jokes only angered him. He barked and snapped at you, and you had to scamper out of his way."

Scowling, Skippy said, "He whimpered at least once."

"No," Burl said.

"I'm sure I remember a whimper," Skippy insisted.

"It was your own," Burl said.

"Surely not," Skippy said.

"Yes."

"Mine?"

"Yes. I'm the elephant, after all, and elephants never forget anything. You can count on my memory of the incident being better than yours."

"I'm so grateful that you set me straight," Skippy said sourly. "Thank you. Thank you so much, so very much. Oh, yes, thank you, thank you."

"You're welcome," Burl said, smiling. He was unaware that the rabbit's thank-yous were scornful and insincere.

A fierce gust of wind moaned at the truck's tailgate. It made the canvas walls and roof flap and flutter against the wooden frame to which they were tied.

"It was *I* who frightened the monster," Patch said. He had pulled a corner of a wool blanket from one of the bales and was wiping the mud and bits of weeds from his clothes and fur. "What a mess I am. I'm so ashamed. Cats must be neat at all times, a good example to less well-groomed animals. Anyway, that dog saw my sword and was frightened of it. Oh, I really am embarrassed by the horrid condition of my costume. I'm disgusting. Please don't look at me. Lower your eyes. Have mercy, please. But the dog, yes, well, the dog saw the sword and realized that I was skilled with the blade, and that's when the fight began to go out of him."

"It's interesting," Burl said, "that cats have memories no better than those of rabbits. My dear Patch, you never had a chance even to poke your sword at the beast. And even if you had gone after him, he would have been unimpressed. In that encounter Butterscotch was the only hero among us."

"I distinctly remember the monster whimpering when I made jokes at his expense," Skippy said.

"Perhaps what you heard," Gibbons said, "was us whimpering at the jokes."

For a minute or two they were silent, listening to the rain and to the hissing of the truck's tires on the wet highway.

Then, one by one, they began to speak of things they had spoken of a hundred times before: their impossible dreams. Burl talked of one day going to Africa and taking his "rightful place" among real elephants. "I can see myself striding majestically across the plains, leading my herd to better grazing and sweeter water."

"But Burl," Butterscotch said gently, "you don't graze or drink water. You're a stuffed-toy elephant."

"Well, sure I am, but that doesn't mean I couldn't lead other elephants to good grass and water."

Gibbons said, "Real elephants would step on you and squash you flat before they even saw you. You're only twenty inches high."

"I'm only twenty inches high," Burl said, "but I could hold my own!"

"I want no part of Africa," Amos said. He sighed dreamily. "But someday it would be nice to live in a pretty little cottage on the edge of the woods and write poetry with a quill pen. Rupert Toon wrote all of his poetry with a quill pen—"

"Sounds as if he wrote it with a sledgehammer," Skippy said.

Amos ignored him. "If I had a cottage and a quill pen, I'm quite sure I could be a good poet."

"What I could be if I had a chance," Skippy said, "is a stand-up comic. I'd be a smash hit in Las Vegas. Do guest spots on TV shows. Maybe have my own series. Get a big house in Beverly Hills next door to Mickey Mouse. Be a *star*." He leaned back against a bale of blankets and crossed his forepaws behind his head. "Yes, sir, I could be a Big-Time Funny Bunny if someone would give me a break."

"I have no interest in fame," Patch said. "What I need to be, what I *long* to be—"

"Is an elephant, of course," Burl said. "In his heart, everyone wants to be an elephant."

"No, a cat," Patch said.

"Cat? But you *are* a cat," Burl said.

"A real cat," Patch said. "I long to be a real cat because real cats lead terribly exciting lives and have great adventures every day. Cats are nature's true swash-bucklers. If I was a real cat, I could chase mousies."

"*Chase* them?" Burl said, obviously horrified. "What a hideous idea. Terrible little creatures, mice. You should avoid them, not chase after them." The elephant shuddered.

"Chase mousies," Patch repeated softly, so pleased by the idea that he had temporarily forgotten about grooming his fur and clothes. He sat as if in a mild trance, staring above Amos's head, apparently thinking about mice.

"What's so great about chasing mousies?" Skippy asked.

"You wouldn't understand."

"Why not?"

"You're not a cat," Patch said. He suddenly noticed the condition of his boots and began to scrub furiously at them with a corner of the wool blanket.

"Well, Patch," Skippy said, "if I do become a Big-Time Funny Bunny and get that Beverly Hills house next door to Mickey Mouse, you can't come to visit if you're going to go chasing my neighbor."

Raising her head from her crossed forepaws and blinking her large brown eyes, Butterscotch said, "I just don't understand this at all. Why aren't you happy to be magic toys? Isn't that enough? Why, it's certainly enough for me. Being a magic toy is a wonderful thing."

"The lady is always the voice of reason," Gibbons said, putting one finger along the side of his snout and squinting at each of the Oddkins. "You'd be well advised to heed what she says."

Butterscotch put her head down on her paws again. "I must admit I regret that I'll never have a litter of pups to nurture and raise. I would enjoy mothering them." She lifted her head again and looked both sad and stern. "But it's not to be. And if you're always dreaming about being something you're not, then you'll never have time to appreciate the joy and wonder of what you *are*."

They were all silent, thinking about what the dog had said.

Amos knew Butterscotch had spoken words of wisdom. Nevertheless he would not mind having a chance to live in a cottage by the edge of the woods, where he could write poetry with a quill pen. . . .

In time the truck stopped. The driver and his partner got out of the cab and hurried away in the rain.

Amos and Patch untied one of the canvas flaps at the rear and led the others out of the truck.

They were among a hundred cars in a dimly lit, deserted parking lot behind a

large white seven-story building with many bright windows. Signs along the rear of the nearest wing said VETERANS' HOSPITAL and STAFF ENTRANCE and EMERGENCY ENTRANCE. Around them, rain drummed on the windshields and roofs of the cars, pattered into puddles, and gurgled down storm drains.

It was not the veterans' hospital that seized the attention of Amos and the other Oddkins. What gripped, astonished, and stunned them was the city that encircled the hospital. On all sides great skyscrapers soared into the rainy night, so tall and massive that the mere sight of them sent a shiver of wonder and fear up the center of Amos's back. The high rises were so huge that they seemed to be tilting forward, looming over the parking lot, in grave danger of crashing down on top of Amos at any moment.

And lights! Everywhere, lights. There must have been a million lighted windows rising up, up, up into the stormy night, vanishing in the mist.

Turning, gazing heavenward, Amos was sure that the tops of the surrounding buildings must arch together and meet at some impossible distance overhead. He grew dizzy. He longed for a cozy cave in which he could curl up and hibernate. Or if not a cave . . . at least a nice, snug, dark toy chest. He closed his eyes, let the rain wash away some of his tension, and told himself to be brave.

"I didn't think it would be so big," Burl said shakily. "Why . . . it must be bigger than all of Africa, bigger than the veldt!"

"No town's too big if you've got talent," Skippy said, straining to sound confident. "If someone here would give me a break, a chance to perform on the stage, I'd have this city at my feet in a week. I'd be the toast of the town. The most famous Big-Time Funny Bunny there ever was."

"Gosh," Butterscotch said, "how will we ever find Mrs. Shannon's toy shop in a place as enormous as this?"

"Cities," Gibbons said, pointing at the skyscrapers with his cane, "are laid out in orderly fashion. Isn't that so, Amos?"

Amos opened his eyes and blinked at the giant buildings and said, "Uh . . . orderly . . . yeah."

"There is a system to the streets, a pattern," Gibbons said. "Isn't that right, Amos?"

"Ummmm . . . pattern . . . yeah."

"Therefore," Gibbons said, "with Amos to lead us, we'll be able to find our way."

Skippy said, "Okay, so lead us, big fella. Lead us out of this miserable rain and into Mrs. Shannon's bright toy shop."

Amos looked left.

He looked right.

He looked forward and back.

"Lead us," Burl said.

"Okeydoke," Amos said. He threw his shoulders back, pushed out his chest, and tried to look like a leader. With great authority he pointed toward the north end of the parking lot. "That way." He set out at a brisk pace between the parked cars, splashing straight through puddles when he encountered them, never hesitating—even though he had no idea where he was going.

3.

Rex and the other Charon toys had to jump off the pipe truck when it stopped at the gates of a construction yard. The only other traffic was a slow-moving car a block behind them, so Rex was sure that he and his comrades had slipped from the truck, under it, through the slanting rain, and into a nearby alleyway without being seen.

Though streetlamps stood at both ends, the middle of the narrow alley was dark. The Charon toys gathered in deep shadows in front of a row of garbage cans.

"This is more like it," Jack Weasel said in his cool, whispery voice, which almost sounded as if it were the storm's voice formed with lips of rain and a tongue of wind.

He streaked away from the others, looped and circled around the center of the alley. His steel wheels clicked and hissed on the wet pavement. When he sped through a puddle he cast up small, twin plumes of water behind him.

"No more muddy fields, no more bumpy forest trails," Jack said gleefully. "The whole city is paved with blacktop, concrete, brick, and cobblestones. Oh, it's *made* for wheeled creatures like me." Giggling, he zoomed to the other toys and braked in front of Rex. "Those soft-bellied Oddkins won't get away from me when I spot them 'cause I can roll twice as fast as they can run. I'll get them for you, Rex. I'll get them for you. I'll run them down."

Stinger had been perched on the rim of a garbage can, but Jack Weasel's excitement had been transmitted to the bee. He took flight, swooped five or six stories straight up, dive-bombed down, darted this way and that, and finally hovered in front of Rex.

"Do you ssssmell them?" Stinger asked in his shrill little voice. His crimson eyes glowed with evil pleasure. "The children? Hmmmmm? Do you ssssmell them all around ussss, Rex?"

Rex smelled them, of course, and he was tempted by the sweetness and innocence of all those children. It would be so easy to find the nearest apartment building, climb a fire escape, pry open the window of a child's bedroom. . . .

"*Thoussssandssss* of children all around ussss," Stinger said. "A city full of children waiting to be sssssssstung."

"I smell them," Lizzie confirmed. She lifted her cigarette holder, and the tip of the plastic cigarette suddenly glowed red-hot. "We could live here in the city forever, hiding out during the day, creeping around at night, tracking down one child after another, tormenting hundreds of them. We'd never run out of prey."

Gear worked his metal hands as if wrenching and pinching the skin of a child. His yellow eyes burned even brighter than the bee's crimson orbs. His jagged metal mouth cracked open. His jaws worked up and down. In his iron voice he said, "Gear wants to tear. Gear wants to break."

Rex shook his head violently, not merely because he was denying them what they wanted but because he was trying to clear his own mind of the overwhelming desire to seek out a child right now and torment it. "No. No, no, no! We will have plenty of time to make children's lives miserable *after* we catch the Oddkins."

"Now, now, now," Jack Weasel said urgently.

"*No!* We must not get sidetracked. First we've got to stop the Oddkins from reaching Mrs. Shannon's toy shop, stop them from letting her know that she's been chosen to be the next toymaker. If she takes over Leben Toys before our kind seize control of the factory, we'll have to return to the subcellar and go back to sleep in our crates for another generation or two. We'll have lost."

"I don't like to lose," said Lizzie.

"Losing is inefficient," said Gear in his hard machinelike voice.

"I hate Oddkins," Jack said.

"Ssssting them, ssssting them," the bee said, doing a series of barrel rolls in the air.

"First the Oddkins," Rex said sternly. "First the Oddkins—and *then* the children." After adjusting his sodden, white bowtie, after smoothing the satin lapels of his rain-soaked tuxedo jacket, Rex raised his black cane and pointed toward the far end of the alley. "The soft-bellied goody-goodies are that way."

He led the Charon toys from one deserted alleyway to another. They were careful to move only through purple-black shadows and through the concealing tentacles of fog that had begun to form near the ground.

Once, when they had to cross a main street, they hid under a bus-stop bench until no traffic was in sight. Then they sprinted for the cover of a couple of big mailboxes on the far side of the broad avenue.

In ten minutes they reached the parking lot behind the veterans' hospital. They found the army truck in which the Oddkins had been riding.

"Where now?" Lizzie asked.

Rex tilted his head one way, then the other, trying to hear the voice of the Dark One. His master did not fail him. He listened, smiled, and said, "Across the parking lot, that way, north."

4.

Victor Bodkins supposed that if people saw him they would think he was a crazy wino, one of those sadly ruined people who lived on the streets of big cities.

He had parked his car near the construction yard where the toys had jumped off the pipe truck. He almost missed seeing them dash into the alley. He would not have spotted them if he had not been looking so hard. From there he pursued his fantastic quarry on foot.

To avoid being seen by the frightful little creatures, Victor scurried from one pool of shadows to another. He hid behind overflowing garbage cans and crawled along filthy alleyways on his hands and knees. The patter, slosh, and gurgle of the rain helped mask the sounds he made.

He was astonished by his own behavior. He had always been a prim, proper, dignified man. In his worst nightmares he had never dreamed of crawling through garbage as if he were a drunken bum.

But he could not stop himself. He had seen impossible things, and he had to know the meaning of them. For his entire adult life—and for most of his childhood, in fact—Victor's imagination had been like a rusted machine, the gears welded together by corrosion. But now suddenly that machine of imagination had come to life. The gears were turning, turning, *whirling*. Victor had lost control; his imagination was racing, unstoppable, dragging him along as if it were a runaway car.

As he scuttled-crept-crawled along the alleyways in pursuit of the toys, his pants became soaked and dirty. He tore his raincoat. Flecks and smears of garbage were stuck to his clothes, unidentifiable stuff so gummy that not even the constant rain could wash it off him. Passing through the edge of the yellowish lightfall from a street lamp, he saw that his hands were grimy. His face was probably no cleaner.

I look like a bum, he thought with dismay. I look like a dirty, tattered old bum.

He did not care what he looked like. The only thing he cared about was keeping track of the toys.

But in the parking lot of the veterans' hospital, he lost them. He was crouched behind a Ford, watching as the toys gathered at the rear of the army truck, but then they headed north, vanishing among the rows of cars. Though Victor raced after them, though he looked down one row of vehicles after another, though he fell to his knees and peered under half the cars in the lot, he could find no trace of the marionettes, the robot, the jack-in-the-box, or the bee.

He was flat on the pavement, squinting into the gloom beneath a Chevrolet, when someone said, "What're you looking for? Are you all right?"

Startled, Victor rolled over and scrambled to his feet.

One of the hospital's doctors was standing nearby, under a big black umbrella. Victor knew the stranger was a doctor because the man's raincoat was open, revealing hospital whites and a dangling stethoscope.

"Are you all right?" the doctor asked.

"There was this robot," Victor said, surprised by the urgency of his own voice. "Yellow eyes and a jagged little mouth."

The doctor frowned. "Robot?"

"Did you see it? Did it pass you? Did you see which way it went? A robot . . . about eighteen inches high."

The doctor stared at him a moment. Then in a gentle, reassuring tone of voice, he said, "Don't you worry. I know all about the little robot."

"You do?" Victor said. "Where did it go?"

"These little robots won't harm anyone."

"It tried to harm me!" Victor assured him.

"Easy now. Easy," the doctor said. "The robots want to be our friends. They come from another planet in tiny little flying saucers, and they want to be our friends."

"I'm serious!" Victor shouted. "You think I'm a crazy old bum, but I'm not. A toy robot. And two marionettes without strings. And a jack-in-the-box. And a flying toy bee. They're chasing a bunch of stuffed animals. I don't know why. Did you see them or not?"

The doctor edged closer and said, "Yes, I saw them, along with a Raggedy Ann doll. They sent me here to bring you to them. They want to talk with you."

Victor backed away from him. "Don't humor me! There wasn't any Raggedy Ann doll! That's silly. You just think I'm crazy, and you want to take me into the hospital. Raggedy Ann doll? Listen, I'm not foolish enough to fall for that!"

He turned away from the doctor and ran toward the far end of the parking lot. He heard the man shouting after him, but he did not look back.

5.

For a moment there was a lull in the storm. The sky closed up, and rain stopped falling.

Patch hoped that his hat would dry out quickly and regain some of its stylish shape.

At the center of a long alleyway was an area lit by a single bulb in a wire security cage above a wooden door. As Amos led his team of furry adventurers to the edge of that light, the cats appeared. Real cats.

The first of the felines made its presence known with a hiss and a sharp, challenging screech.

Amos, Gibbons, and Butterscotch gasped in surprise.

Startled, in search of the source of the sound, Skippy whirled so suddenly that his huge floppy ears wrapped around his face, covering his mouth and leaving only one eye revealed. "Mmmphhh spmmmph," he said.

"It must be a lion," Burl said, "just like on the veldt."

"Mmmmphhh."

The cat was above them, crouched on the first landing of an iron fire escape. It was big, coal-black, with glowing eyes. Judging by its angry tone, it wanted to know why they were trespassing in its territory.

As if called forth by the cry of their leader above, two other cats appeared from behind an overflowing green dumpster and an empty, wooden packing crate. One was gray. One was yellow-orange with tigerlike markings. Both were large and scruffy.

Patch was mortified. He would have blushed if he had not been a stuffed toy and therefore incapable of blushing. He stepped forward and said, "Brothers, fellow cats, dear kin of mine, please accept my apologies for my dreadful appearance. I am quite ashamed. But we've come a long way under difficult circumstances. And although I have struggled continuously to keep myself well groomed, I'm afraid I've not been entirely successful."

The gray and orange cats halted ten feet from him. They crouched, their tails and heads held low, their gazes riveted on Patch.

He said, "I assure you that usually my cavalier boots are well polished, my trousers pressed, my shirt spotless. Ordinarily my hat is not soaked and drooping, nor is my fur matted with mud." He peered thoughtfully at his tense kin and added: "In fact, I am usually far better groomed than either of you. If you'll excuse my saying so, neither of you is a good example to young kittens."

All three cats—the one above and the two in front of Patch—hissed angrily. One of them growled deep in its throat.

"Oh, no offense intended, of course," Patch said quickly. "But after all, we cats must uphold our noble reputation for being fussy about our personal appearance."

Having unwrapped his ears from his face, Skippy stepped forward and said, "Listen, Douglas Furball, these guys are alley cats, feline hoodlums."

"Don't call me Douglas Furball," Patch said, "or I'll tie your ears to your ankles and roll you along like a hoop."

"Uncle Isaac—"

"Yes, yes, I know," Patch said, "Uncle Isaac called me Douglas Furball because I shared his taste for those old Douglas Fairbanks movies about swashbucklers. But only Uncle Isaac could call me that. No one else. You understand?"

"Touchy, touchy," Skippy said.

The alley cats growled and advanced one step, then another.

Patch noticed traces of foul garbage on their whiskers and was revolted.

Behind Patch, Amos said, "Everyone form a circle with your backs to one another. Be prepared to defend yourselves."

"No!" Patch said, drawing the rubber sword from the scabbard on his hip. "Butterscotch dealt with the nasty mongrel who was an embarrassment to her kind, so I should deal with these poor excuses for cats." He wrinkled his nose in disgust. "Look at them—badly groomed, garbage-eating, unmannered ruffians of the worst kind."

The tiger-striped cat leaped forward.

Patch slapped it across the face with his rubber sword.

The mangy villain squealed, whirled, and retreated in fear and confusion.

On the fire escape, the black cat screeched angrily and started down the iron steps.

"Uh," Skippy said, "maybe they're just cross because their lives are so grim. Poor homeless creatures without television sets and no chance ever to go to the movies. Maybe they're desperately in need of some first-rate entertainment. A few jokes might make them feel more friendly, more—"

Amos rushed in behind the rabbit, grabbed his ears, wrapped them around his head again to cover his mouth, and pulled him backward.

"Mmmmphhh spmmmphhh!"

The gray cat sprinted forward.

Patch danced nimbly to his left and used the flat, broad side of his sword on the beast's flank as it darted past him.

The gray cat squalled angrily.

Its courage regained, the tiger cat sprinted at Patch once more.

Patch stepped forward to meet it, brandishing his rubber blade.

The cat halted but took a swipe at him with one paw, leaving a two-inch tear in his trousers.

"You villain! You black-hearted fiend!" cried Patch. "You've ripped my costume, and for that you'll pay dearly!"

He launched himself at the tiger-striped ruffian, slapping it repeatedly with his sword, driving it backward. But then the gray one attacked him from behind, leaping on him, knocking him off his feet. And the black cat, having descended the fire escape, was upon him too. The four of them rolled back and forth, squealing and hissing and screeching.

A claw dug at Patch's face. One of his painted glass eyes popped loose, and he could see only half as well as before. Abruptly—and reluctantly—Patch realized that he was no match for an entire pack of alley cats.

Before he could cry for help, however, the other Oddkins came to his rescue. Burl trumpeted in a voice that was similar to, though quieter than, that of a real elephant, and he stomped his stumpy feet. He shouted, "Rogue elephant! Rogue elephant on the rampage! Look out, you mangy cats, there's a rogue elephant loose in this alleyway! Everybody's gonna get squished if they don't watch out. Squish-squish! Squish-squish!"

Amos waded into the tangled mass of cats, swinging a foot-long piece of wood that he had picked up from beside one of the broken packing crates. Patch saw that Amos was using the makeshift sword with little grace; actually, the bear was wielding it more like a club. But right now there was no time for *style*. The only thing that mattered was survival.

With his cane, Gibbons hacked at the three cats.

Barking, Butterscotch leaped into the fray.

Skippy suddenly appeared out of the low fog, waving his arms and shouting, "Booga-booga-booga-booga!"

"Squish-squish! Squish-squish!"

"Arf, arf, arf!"

"Booga-booga-boooooooga!"

The alley cats were bold creatures, but they had never been faced with such a group of unpredictable adversaries. Retreating from the blows administered by Amos and Gibbons, confused and frightened by the strange cries of the rabbit, intimidated by the barking dog and the elephant, they fled at last.

Though he was now missing one eye, Patch leaped to his feet and raised his sword. He called after the departing hoodlums: "You'd make better rats than cats, you worthless vermin!"

"Booga-booga-booga!" Skippy added.

6.

Nick Jagg was sitting on one of the wooden benches in the terminal's main lounge, waiting for the bus, when the night clerk called to him from the ticket counter. "Hey, bad news, I'm afraid. The bus you're waiting for has broken down. There's going to be a three-hour delay before the next one."

"Three hours?" Jagg said irritably.

"Sorry," the clerk said, and shrugged.

From his conversation with the creature in the men's room mirror, Jagg had gotten the idea that he must assume the role of toymaker as quickly as possible. His mission was urgent. Now he wondered how he was going to get to the city to buy the toy factory tonight.

He looked worriedly toward the front doors of the terminal. As his gaze fixed on the rainy night beyond, a bus pulled up at the curb. It was black and strange looking.

The sound of the brakes drew the clerk's attention away from the book he was reading. "What line's that? Nothing's due in now."

Jagg picked up the money-filled suitcase and walked to the front doors of the terminal. He peered through the rain-speckled glass.

Outside, the doors of the night-black bus opened, but no one got out of it.

Jagg knew this ride had been sent just for him—sent by the same creature he had seen in the mirror.

"That's not Greyhound, is it?" the clerk asked. "Not Trailways, either, is it?"

Without answering, Jagg pushed through the doors and stood for a moment on the sidewalk, in the rain, looking up at the bus. The windows were all tinted, so he could see nothing of the interior.

He went to the open doors, climbed three metal steps, and came face to face with the driver. The man was as pale as new-fallen snow, with cold gray eyes. He wore a black suit, an equally black shirt, and a black tie. He nodded at Jagg and closed the doors.

Jagg saw that the bus was empty. He went to a seat in the middle and settled down by the window as the vehicle got underway.

Once they were out of town and on the main highway, they moved very fast, even though the rain had turned to sleet and was painting a crust of ice on the road.

7.

The Oddkins could not find the painted glass bauble that had been Patch's left eye. It was flat on one side rather than completely round, so it could not have rolled far. They looked under and behind the green dumpster. They searched around the large packing crates and all along the litter-strewn alley, but the bright green bit of glass was nowhere to be seen.

Patch was not in agony, for he did not have the capacity for serious physical pain. He could feel emotions like fear, love, joy, and sadness. But being just a stuffed-toy cat, he was not much bothered by heat, cold, or other physical sensations.

His vision was impaired, of course. He could see only out of his right eye, which left him with a blind side that might prove to be dangerous in future battles.

However, the thing that most concerned Patch was his appearance. He turned to the trash dumpster and leaned against it as his friends gathered behind him. He averted his face, trying not to let them see him. "Oh, just look at me. No,

don't! Don't look at me. I'm an awful sight. Wet, filthy, with a tear in my trousers. And just look at this soggy, drooping hat. No, don't! Don't look! If you have any compassion, don't stare. What a wretched mess I am, unfit to call myself a cat.''

''You look fine to me,'' Amos said.

''Are you *looking* at me?'' Patch demanded, still turned away from them, hiding his face.

''I don't see anything disgusting about you,'' Burl said. ''A bit battered, sure, but there's something noble about that.''

''Are *you* looking at me too?'' Patch wailed.

''I think you look swell,'' Skippy said. ''Heroic.''

''Dashing,'' Gibbons said.

''You're *all* looking at me!'' Patch said, and he stamped his feet in frustration.

Amos said, ''Please, Patch, don't worry yourself like this. You're no embarrassment to yourself or to cats in general. In those old movies, Douglas Fairbanks didn't always look as if he had just stepped out of a dry cleaner's, did he?''

''Well . . . no,'' Patch agreed, still facing the dumpster.

''In fact,'' Amos said, ''sometimes, after a big battle, he was all sweaty, his hair was messed up, and his clothes were dirty and even torn. Isn't that true?''

''Hmmmm,'' Patch said thoughtfully.

''Yet he was still a hero even when his appearance was less than satisfactory.''

Butterscotch said, ''Patch, we all like to look our best, but the way we look is not as important as *what we are.* What's inside is more important than what's outside. And inside, you're a good cat, maybe the finest cat who ever was— brave, reliable, honest, and true. And all your friends can see those wonderful qualities no matter how wet, muddy, and tattered you may be.''

Slowly, shyly, Patch turned away from the dumpster and faced the others, revealing his disfigured, one-eyed face. ''How ugly am I?'' he asked shakily.

"Oh," said Skippy, "easily as ugly as Cary Grant. Easily as ugly as Tom Selleck. But not as ugly as Douglas Fairbanks."

"But," Patch said, confused, "none of *them* was ugly at all!"

"That's my point," Skippy said. "You're no more ugly than Gable or Grant or Fairbanks."

Patch gave him a one-eyed blink of surprise. He looked at each of his friends and saw no disgust in any of them. His dirty, rumpled, one-eyed appearance did not seem to shock or repel them.

"Well, now that I look at you closely," Skippy said, pretending to preen himself, "perhaps you are a bit uglier than *me*, but then . . . who isn't?"

Patch laughed, and so did the other Oddkins.

Grinning, Skippy put on a stand-up comic voice: "You're a great audience, folks. I love ya. I really do. I want to take you all home with me. I love ya."

Butterscotch had also been injured in the battle. Her right forepaw was cut, and some stuffing was blossoming from the tear in her fabric. With every step she took, more stuffing bulged out of her leg.

Somehow, Amos knew that it was dangerous for an Oddkin to lose too much of his inner material. He did not know what would happen to Butterscotch if she lost a lot of stuffing, and he certainly did not want to find out.

"That's all right," she said softly. "I can favor the leg and walk on three feet. I can limp along just fine. If I don't put my weight on the foot, no more stuffing will come out."

Amos shook his head. "Nope. On three legs, you'd be too slow to keep up with us. And we've got to get to Mrs. Shannon's place as quickly as possible. Let's find something we can use to bind up your wound."

Among the trash in the alleyway, they turned up a few rags. Together, Amos and Burl tore one of those scraps into long strips. They used two lengths of cloth to wrap the wound in Butterscotch's forepaw, preventing any more stuffing from dribbling out of her, and allowing her to walk without a limp.

A while ago the rain suddenly stopped falling, but now it began to pour down again as hard as ever. This time bits of sleet were mixed in. The hard, tiny pellets of ice tapped almost musically against the metal dumpster and ticked-pinged-clinked on the iron steps of the fire escape.

Leaning forward, putting his burly head down to resist the force of the wind and rain and sleet, Amos led his friends to the end of the alleyway. They moved cautiously out onto the puddled sidewalk along a major street. It was a commercial district of clothing, record, furniture, and gift stores.

At the moment, thanks to the late hour and the storm, no traffic was in sight. But Amos warned the other Oddkins to be prepared to dash for cover the instant that they saw a car or—far less likely—a pedestrian. There were many places to hide in the recessed entranceways of the dark, deserted shops by which they passed.

Amos was still not sure where he was going, but he began to feel that he was not wandering aimlessly. Something was drawing him along a particular route, guiding him ever closer to Mrs. Shannon's toy shop. Maybe what he felt was the spirit of Uncle Isaac Bodkins gently tugging him in the right direction.

Some of the stores were illuminated by nightlights. From time to time Amos looked up to see, as best he could, what sort of merchandise was displayed in the windows. The eighth or tenth time that he glanced up, he was stunned by what he saw: books.

Books, books, hundreds of books!

Being a bookish bear, a lover of poetry and Dickens, Amos was overcome by his first encounter with a bookstore. He froze for a moment in disbelief, then dashed to the window—which was just low enough to the sidewalk to allow him to press his face and paws against the glass.

Books!

Gibbons, scholar that he was, accompanied Amos to the window. He peered with considerable interest at the wares that the store chose to display. "Ummm . . . yes . . . a rare-book store. Some nice volumes. That looks like a superb copy of *The Wind in the Willows.*"

"Never heard of it," Amos said.

"Oh, an excellent story," Gibbons said.

"What's it about?"

"Mainly, it's about an adventurous and daring toad."

"Toad? Gosh, I think I'd like to read a book about a toad."

The other Oddkins, less interested in literature, hung back, watching the avenue for traffic.

"*Pinocchio,*" Gibbons said. "That one's about a marionette that comes to life."

"Sounds good, too," Amos said, "though I'd still prefer the tale of the daring toad, I think."

"*Charlotte's Web.* Now that's about a pig, a spider, and a little girl."

"No toad?"

"There can't be a toad in every book," Gibbons said.

Skippy joined them and said, "Hey, you guys, we're wasting time. Let's get a move on."

"Books are never a waste of time," Amos said solemnly. "Don't you know what Rubert Toon said about books?"

Skippy, Gibbons, and the other Oddkins all groaned at the mention of Rupert Toon, but Amos could not be stopped. He stepped back from the shop window,

stood with his legs spread wide. He recited the Toon poem with much dramatic gesturing:

> I think books are really dandy,
> better than a box of candy,
> better than a brand-new suit,
> better than a horn to toot,
> better than a rubber boot.
> Just as nests are full of birds,
> books are always full of words—

"This is terrible," Burl moaned. "Worse than being trapped in a room with a hundred mice."

"This Toon ought to be arrested," Skippy said. "There should be poetry police."

> Just as cows go 'round in herds,
> books are full of herds of words—

"Please stop," Patch begged. "Please, oh, please. If I had been lucky enough to lose one ear instead of one eye, I'd have to listen to only half of this!"

> Entertainment, learning—gadzooks:
> all of it can be found in books.

"He stopped!" Skippy said. "I think he's done. I think it's over. Oh, thank heaven, the poem is ended."

"I didn't think I was going to survive that one," Burl said.

"More dangerous than those alley cats," Patch said.

"Well," Butterscotch said, "at least it rhymed."

Before Amos had a chance to defend the poetry of Rupert Toon, he was startled by a tuxedo-clad marionette that dashed out of the mouth of an alley only sixty feet away and skidded to a halt.

"Hey, Gibbons, look," Amos said. "It's Pinocchio!"

"I don't think so," Gibbons said ominously. "Pinocchio was a *good* marionette, and this one looks nasty."

Another marionette appeared, then a jack-in-the-box, a flying toy bee, and a robot. They gathered on the sidewalk, the bee hovering over their heads, and they faced the Oddkins.

"Uh-oh," Skippy said. "Bad guys."

"What should we do?" Butterscotch asked.

"Fight!" Patch said, drawing his sword.

"Teach them a lesson," Gibbons said.

"Squish them!" Burl said.

"Make them sorry they were ever assembled," Skippy said.

Sixty feet away, the jack-in-the-box emitted a piercing, mad giggle.

"Run!" Amos said.

"I see why Uncle Isaac made *you* the leader," Burl said.

Following Amos, the Oddkins turned and ran, slipping and sliding on the sleet-skinned sidewalk.

8.

Victor Bodkins was surprised by how deserted the city could seem late on a winter's night when the weather was bad enough to keep most people at home. He splashed down empty alleyways, crossed deserted streets.

Shortly after midnight, looking for some sign of the toys, he even walked up the center of a sleet-lashed avenue, scanning the entranceways and the narrow spaces between buildings on both sides. The only vehicles he saw were two street-maintenance trucks that crossed on intersecting boulevards, spreading rock salt behind them to melt the treacherous ice.

He was cold and weary. His legs ached. His palms hurt, for he had slipped a couple of times and had scraped his hands on the pavement when he had attempted unsuccessfully to break his fall.

He felt feverish. He should go home, take a hot shower, eat some soup, swallow a couple of aspirins, and go to bed. Maybe he had been feverish earlier than he had realized. Maybe he had been coming down with the flu or some other ailment when he had been on his way to his uncle's toy factory, and maybe he had hallucinated his encounters with the living toys. Maybe none of it had been real.

What madness has overcome me? he wondered.

Still wondering, he crossed the street, waded through the thick icy slush in the gutter, and stepped up onto the sidewalk. He stood for a moment, letting the sleet tap on his bare head. Glistening beads of ice slid down his rumpled, filthy raincoat.

"Go home," he told himself. "You went temporarily mad, but there's still hope for you if you'll just go home. There's no magic in the world, Victor. You've always known that there's no magic. No such thing as living toys, for heaven's sake! Owning the toy factory has done this to you. You inherited it only hours ago, but somehow it's put a curse on you, deranged you. The factory is cursed—yes, that's it—and anyone who owns it is cursed to behave like a child, just as poor Isaac behaved all his life and just as you have been behaving tonight. You must go home, get some rest, and sell the factory as soon as possible, before the cursed place corrupts you the way that it corrupted Isaac. There is no magic in the world. Life is hard, unpleasant. You must act responsibly, be an adult. Really now."

9.

Amos looked back at the evil toys and saw they were gaining.

However, in its eagerness to attack, the bee flew head-on into the bookstore sign that overhung the sidewalk. The impact was like a gunshot, and the bee fell straight down to the sidewalk.

The other toys rushed past the bee, not even pausing to see how badly it had been hurt. The jack-in-the-box was in front of the pack. His hard-edged steel wheels cut through the patches of ice on the sidewalk, so he did not slip and slide.

Amos stretched his stumpy legs, trying to run faster. Squinting into the sleety, misty night ahead, he searched for a refuge.

Half a minute later, they were in front of a fire station, where one of the three big garage doors was raised. Inside, two enormous red fire trucks stood at the ready, flanking an empty bay where a third truck ought to have been. The soft, warm light of the station looked inviting.

"In there!" Amos said, and he led the Oddkins through the open garage door, past the truck, seeking a safe place.

They almost rushed straight through a doorway that connected the firehouse garage with a back room. At the threshold, startled by voices and a burst of laughter, Amos looked up and saw that the room was occupied by firemen playing cards. Apparently one of them had just told a joke. Fortunately none of them was looking toward the door. Amos lurched sideways, out of sight.

Gibbons, Burl, Patch, and Butterscotch followed.

Evidently thinking that he was the cause of the laughter, Skippy stopped on the threshold and grinned happily, standing in plain sight. He struck a comic pose, then another, and when the firemen's laughter continued, the rabbit took a bow.

Amos reached out and grabbed Skippy, pulled him into the shadows, and whispered, "Keep out of sight!"

"They want an encore," Skippy said.

"Quiet!"

"My public calls."

At the front of the building, the jack-in-the-box rolled out of the sleet-filled night and into the garage.

"We're trapped," Gibbons said.

"Quickly," Amos whispered. "Get up onto the fire truck before he sees us."

They hurried around the back of the vehicle, to the other side, where the jack-in-the-box could not as easily spot them. As silently as possible, they climbed—Butterscotch and Patch jumped—onto the steel running board, which was divided into three sections. Gibbons, Burl, and Skippy were at the back of the truck. Patch and Butterscotch were on a short section of running board farther forward, just behind the front wheel. And Amos was alone, on an even shorter perch just behind the front bumper.

They wanted to climb higher, squirm in among the hoses and other equipment until they were completely out of sight. But before they could go any farther, they heard the hissing, clicking wheels of the jack-in-the-box as it rolled under the truck in search of them. They dared not move now, for fear that they would make a sound that would give away their position.

Softly, softly, the tiny wheels went *click-hissssss-click-hissssss*.

From under the truck, the jack-in-the-box whispered eerily: "Hello there, soft-bellied ones. Where are you? Come out and play. Come out and play with old Jack Weasel."

Click-hissssss-click-hissssss-click.

Amos stood very still, hoping with all his might that Isaac Bodkins was watching over them right now.

"Come say hello to old Jack Weasel," the evil creature hissed from beneath the truck.

Click-hissssss . . .

"What's the matter, soft-bellied ones? Are you afraid I'll bite?" Jack Weasel issued a thin, insane giggle.

Click-hissssss-click . . .

Below Amos's perch and directly in front of him, Jack Weasel rolled out from under the fire truck. Amos was looking down on the back of the jack-in-the-box's head, no more than a foot above the creature.

Weasel used his gloved hands to push himself another foot or two along the floor, which was wet from rain and sleet that had blown through the open garage door. The water-filmed concrete was highly reflective, almost like a mirror, so there appeared to be a pair of jack-in-the-boxes, one of them rolling along upside-down beneath the other.

Halting about three feet from the fire truck, Jack Weasel looked slowly to his left, then slowly to his right, giving Amos a good view of both frightening profiles. He stared across the empty bay at the second truck in the three-bay garage, studying the shadows around and under that vehicle.

Amos dared not move even one paw. He desperately hoped that the other Oddkins were equally rigid. The slightest movement would surely catch Jack Weasel's attention even though he was not looking in their direction; he would spot motion from the corner of his eye, and that would be the end of the Oddkins' good luck.

"Oh, I wish I had a soft-bellied Oddkin to eat," Weasel said with frightening, whispery urgency.

Amos shivered violently.

Jack Weasel wrapped his arms around himself and giggled softly. "Oh, my. Oh, I just can't take it any more. It tickles me too much. Mr. Bear, I saw you the moment I rolled out from under the truck." He wheeled around to face them. "I saw your face reflected in the floor as you leaned out to peer down at me."

Amos had never seen such horrible eyes as Jack Weasel's. The pupil of one was large and red, the other small and green. Both eyes were round, bulging madly from the clownlike face.

Weasel giggled again and rolled directly to the truck but not to Amos, heading instead to the second section of the running board, where Patch and Butterscotch were perched. "Hello, pretty doggy. How about coming down and playing with old Jack Weasel?"

Patch brandished his rubber sword at Weasel and said, "Get away from us, you foul devil."

Weasel grabbed the end of the sword and tried to wrench it out of Patch's hand.

Struggling mightily, Patch managed to hold on to the weapon.

Abruptly Jack Weasel let go of the sword and snatched instead at Butterscotch's wounded paw. His arms were just long enough to reach her.

She gasped when he seized her paw and tried to pull free, but Weasel was stronger.

In the back room, the card-playing firemen laughed again, unaware of the strange drama being played out in the adjacent garage. Amos wished he could call to the firemen for help, but he knew that he must avoid being seen by adults.

Patch chopped at the jack-in-the-box's arms with the rubber sword but to no avail.

"Going to pull you down into my box and close the lid, doggy," said Jack Weasel to Butterscotch. "Going to pull you inside here with me, doggy, in here where it's ever so dark and deep, deeper than you'd think, and I'm going to crunch you up with these big wooden teeth of mine."

Amos was just about to jump down to the floor and rush Weasel, try to tilt him over, off his wheels. But then he heard a small, cruel voice from the front of the garage:

"Get them. Destroy them."

Looking toward the voice, Amos saw the male marionette standing with his female companion and the robot just inside the open garage door. The bee was nowhere in sight.

Letting go of Butterscotch, Jack Weasel turned toward the tuxedo-clad marionette. In an eerie, worshipful tone, he said, "I found them, Rex. See? See? I found them for you. Isn't that good, Rex? Didn't I do good?"

Rex and his hideous companions were prepared for battle. The robot's yellow eyes blazed brighter; it flexed its dangerous-looking metal hands. The female marionette raised a cigarette, the tip of which instantly changed from black to red-hot. Rex raised his fancy cane, and a sharp blade popped from the end of it. The terrible trio moved farther into the firehouse.

Rex looked directly at Amos and said, "You're finished. *Our* time has come."

"Don't be so sure," Amos said bravely.

But he thought: *We're doomed. We can't chase these guys off as easily as we did the alley cats.*

Barking erupted behind him.

For a moment Amos wondered how Butterscotch had acquired this new, louder, meaner voice. But when he turned, he saw that a real dog had come into the garage from the back room where, out of sight, the firemen were no doubt still playing cards.

The dog, a Dalmatian, seemed confused. It looked at the Oddkins where they perched on the fire truck, and it almost smiled, sensing that they were friendly types. But when it looked at Jack Weasel and at the other toys near the open garage door, it clearly sensed that *they* were no more friendly than a nest of rattlesnakes.

"Be a good dog," Butterscotch said, "and make your mother proud of her pup. Chase off these nasty toys."

Jack Weasel giggled and rolled toward the dog. "Back off, you stupid cur. We've already dealt with one of your kind tonight. Get in our way, and we'll make sausages of you."

Challenged, the black-spotted Dalmatian did not retreat but leaped straight at the jack-in-the-box.

Weasel was surprised, as if he expected creatures of good heart always to shiver and flee at the sight of his evil leer. With a thin squeal of fear, he spun away from the dog and raced for the open door.

There's a lesson here, Amos thought as he watched the drama below him. *Maybe bad toys become more dangerous when you run away from them than they are when you stand up to them. Hmmmmm.*

As the angry dog pursued Weasel, Rex stepped forward, raising his stiletto-tipped cane.

The robot clanked a couple of steps forward, too, working its jagged mouth.

"Ashes?" one of the firemen called from the back room. "What are you barking at, Ashes?"

Ashes the Dalmatian skidded to a stop on the concrete floor. He hesitated, glanced at the door of the card room, then leaped at Weasel again, snarling and barking.

"Ashes!" the fireman called, and his voice was closer than before. He was coming out to the garage to see what had so excited the dog.

The two marionettes and the robot seemed to be having second thoughts about confronting the Dalmatian, and the approach of the fireman convinced them to retreat. The bad toys turned and vanished into the sleety night, with Jack Weasel and the firehouse dog close behind.

A tall, dark-haired fireman with a mustache entered the garage from the card room.

Amos at once pretended to be an ordinary stuffed animal, as lifeless as a cooked turnip. He hoped the other Oddkins would be wise enough to do the same.

The fireman hurried past them, taking no notice whatsoever that a collection of stuffed animals was perched on the fire truck. He also disappeared into the night, calling the Dalmatian's name.

"Quickly!" Amos said. "Under the truck. Hide!"

The Oddkins jumped, climbed, and tumbled down. They scurried into the shadows beneath the big vehicle, where they gathered in a close circle in hopes of taking courage from one another.

"Those other toys," Burl whispered. "You think they're from the subcellar, like you were telling us, Gibbons?"

"Well," Skippy said, "they sure weren't the kind Santa Claus would put under a tree!"

"Definitely from the subcellar," Gibbons said. "Products of the previous owner, the one before Uncle Isaac. Charon toys."

"With them after us," Patch said, "getting to Mrs. Shannon's toy shop is *really* going to be an adventure."

"Don't sound so pleased," Skippy said, frowning. "You may be a swashbuckler, but I'm not. I'm just a Funny Bunny, and I'm *never* going to get my star on the Hollywood Walk of Fame if those characters get their hands on me. Why, they look more dangerous than a pack of movie-studio accountants."

"What's that mean?" Butterscotch asked.

Skippy shrugged. "I don't know. I heard someone say that on TV, and it got a laugh."

"Sssshhh," Amos warned. "Someone's coming."

The mustachioed fireman returned with the Dalmatian. Melting sleet dripped off both of them. The man pushed a button to roll down the garage door.

Oh, no, thought Amos. *How do we get out of here now?*

"Whatever got you so excited, Ashes?" The fireman stooped to stroke and pat the dog. "Never heard you bark so mean before. You going to behave yourself?"

The Dalmatian curled up on the floor, put its head on its paws, and whined softly, as if in apology.

When the fireman returned to his card game, Ashes rose, padded to the fire engine, and peered at where the Oddkins had gathered in the gloom. He chuffed in a friendly fashion and smiled at them.

"Good dog," Butterscotch said. "A credit to your litter and to your mother's name."

The Dalmatian seemed to understand her. He got on his belly, wriggled beneath the truck, and poked his nose at each of the six Oddkins, sniffing them in turn.

"What if he decides we're good to eat?" Skippy asked.

"Ashes is a *nice* dog," Butterscotch said impatiently.

"He won't eat me," Burl said confidently as he endured the dog's snuffling inspection. "Dogs don't eat elephants . . . at least not very often . . . I think."

"But real dogs eat rabbits," Skippy said.

"They also like a taste of cat now and then," Patch said as the Dalmatian's attention turned to him.

"This is foolish talk," Amos said.

"Easy for you to keep cool," Skippy said. "Dogs don't eat bears, any more than they eat elephants."

"It would be stupid for a dog to eat an elephant," Burl said uneasily. "It would surely get indigestion from the tusks."

"I'm certain Ashes is a vegetarian," Amos said, trying to allay his friends' fear.

"Besides," Gibbons said, "no dog I ever heard of would eat an animal made out of cloth, bits of leather, and cotton stuffing."

"He's a nice dog," Butterscotch repeated, and she put one paw on the Dalmatian's much larger paw as he sniffed at her.

Amos was the last to receive the dog's inspection. As he was being sniffed at, he said, "Listen, pooch, we must get out of here and be on our way. There's very important business we've got to attend to before dawn. Can you show us a way out? Hmmmm? Do you know a way out of here now that the big door's been closed?"

Skippy said, "There's something you need to know, Amos."

"What?"

"Real dogs can't talk."

"I already know that," Amos said. "But maybe he can understand. He seems to understand the fireman, so maybe he'll understand me. Can you show us a way out, fella? Hmmmm? Can you help us get out of here and on our way?"

Ashes stared into Amos's eyes for a long moment, then wriggled from beneath the fire truck and padded across the garage. He stopped and looked back at them as if to ask why they were not following him.

"Come on," Amos said. "Let's see where he's going."

Ashes led them out of the garage, along a hallway, to the firehouse's rear door. The bottom half of the door was fitted with a hinged panel big enough to allow the dog passage. The Dalmatian squeezed through, and the Oddkins followed him into a fenced yard behind the firehouse.

The dead winter grass glistened with a thin coat of ice from the storm. Sleet ticked off every surface and was slowly but surely draping a cold, transparent curtain over the chain link fence that enclosed the property.

Ashes led them to a dark, back corner of the lot, under a leafless oak. There, he set to digging industriously at the half-frozen earth, tearing up clumps of dirt until he had excavated a passageway under the fence.

"I told you he was a nice dog," Butterscotch said. "And smart too. Very smart."

Ashes panted happily.

Frowning at the Dalmatian, Amos said, "Funny . . . but I have the oddest feeling that Uncle Isaac is close right now. Very close indeed."

The Dalmatian blinked at him and smiled even more broadly.

"Let's go," Skippy said, "before those nasty toys find us."

The rabbit slipped under the fence, followed by Butterscotch, Gibbons, Patch, and Burl. Beyond was an icy alleyway.

Amos went last of all. Then he paused to look back into the Dalmatian's eyes one last time. He was searching for some indication that Isaac Bodkins's spirit had temporarily settled in this firehouse mascot.

Peering back through the fence at the Dalmatian, who chose not to follow them, Burl said, "Ummm . . . listen, I'm sorry for thinking you might want to munch on us."

"Me too," said Skippy, appearing at Burl's side. "Someday, when I'm a famous Funny Bunny, if you can work up a trick or two, I'll be glad to give you a job on my TV show."

"Come on," Amos said. "I get the feeling that those bad toys are close by and closing in."

The Oddkins hurried together along the dark alleyway. Every time that Amos looked back, the Dalmatian was still at the fence, watching after them.

4

TOO MUCH
ADVENTURE

1.

A park full of many trees and grassy lawns lay at the center of the city. Amos was drawn to that quiet place, and somehow he knew that he must lead the Oddkins through that open land in order to get to Mrs. Shannon's toy shop.

"Not as nice as the veldt," Burl said, looking around at the park as they passed through it, "but nice enough."

Sleet was still falling. Ice encased the bare black branches of the trees. Each blade of winter-brown grass was frozen stiff. The walkways were slippery in places, and the black iron lampposts were beginning to grow transparent beards of ice.

After repeatedly falling down and after struggling against the forceful wind, the Oddkins paused to rest under a long, narrow, roofed pavilion that sheltered a section of the walkway. There, the sleet could not reach them, though the wind still puffed through the open walls.

Behind the pavilion was a very high fence of sturdy iron bars. Beyond the fence, in the shadows, was a large barnlike structure, almost hidden by the night and the falling sleet. Amos noticed the place but did not give it special attention.

The Oddkins were partially cloaked in ice. They began taking it off in pieces, as if they were a group of small, furry knights stripping off their armor.

Skippy said, "I don't understand why the new magic toymaker couldn't have lived next door to Uncle Isaac Bodkins. It would have been a lot more convenient."

"This is a noble quest," Gibbons said. "Everyone knows that noble quests must always be difficult."

"Why must they always be difficult?" Amos asked.

Gibbons thought about that a moment, then put one finger beside his long snout. "Perhaps because any job that's too easy is not worthwhile. Perhaps hard work, challenging work, the kind of work that tests us and demands the best of us, is the most valuable."

"Why?" Amos asked.

"Well . . . because hard work and difficult challenges teach us not to give up easily. They teach us that accomplishing things in life requires dedication, sweat, and patience."

"We Oddkins have dedication and patience," Butterscotch said, "but none of us can sweat."

"And a good thing too!" Patch said. "Just imagine what a mess I'd be if, aside from being soaked and dirty and torn, I was also stinking of sweat." He shuddered.

"Eeep," Skippy said.

Busy cracking ice off his stubby legs, Amos did not glance up at the rabbit. "What did you say, Skippy?"

"Eeep."

"What's that supposed to mean?"

"Eeep, eeep," Skippy said.

"Eeep," Butterscotch said.

"Double eeep," Patch said.

Even Gibbons said, "Eeep!"

Frowning, Amos finally stopped picking ice off his legs and turned to see what they were talking about.

Apparently there was a zoo in the park. A real, live elephant stood at the high iron fence behind the covered walkway, evidently having come out of the unlighted barnlike structure that Amos had noticed earlier.

It was not only the hugest creature Amos had ever seen but far bigger than he had ever *imagined* an elephant could be. Each of its ears was as large as an army tent. Its tusks were the size of small trees. From Amos's point of view, the creature's rippled trunk looked like a very long, grand staircase leading up to its mammoth brow.

Amos said, "Eeep."

"We're perfectly safe," Gibbons said. "I'm quite sure we are. Yes, yes. Quite sure. Those iron bars will hold him back."

"Looks to me like he could snap those bars in a minute," said Patch.

"In a second," Butterscotch said.

"And then squish us," Skippy said. "That's what elephants like to do. Squish things. Squish-squish. We've learned that from Burl."

Wide-eyed with astonishment, Burl moved slowly toward the bars. "He doesn't want to squish anyone. He's friendly."

Amos stared up into the giant's small, curious eye, which was surrounded by wrinkles and bright with what might have been ancient wisdom. He decided that Burl was right. This was a friendly fellow.

But Skippy was not as easily convinced. "Friendly? How can you possibly tell?"

"Because . . . I'm like him," Burl said. "We're brothers, he and I. We share the long, proud history of our kind."

The real elephant swayed slightly from side to side and rolled its enormous head, as if agreeing with Burl.

"I'll bet he once lived out on the veldt," Burl said, his voice trembling with awe. "Lived under the stars, roaming the plains, with his mate at his side—we mate for life, you know—and with his herd following respectfully behind him. Oh, look at him, how huge and magnificent he is, how beautiful and noble!"

The elephant's enormous trunk snaked through two of the bars and curled toward little Burl.

Burl stepped forward and touched his own small trunk to the tip of his real-life cousin's much greater nose. They stood very still, staring at each other, trunk to trunk in special communion.

No longer afraid, Amos and the other Oddkins gathered around Burl, staring in tingly amazement at the zoo elephant.

Butterscotch said, "Seeing this creature, I think I feel some of the wonder and

magic that people must feel when they accidentally get a good glimpse of a living Oddkin."

Amos knew what Butterscotch meant. He said, "God's world is *full* of magic, isn't it? Not just the secret kind of magic of which we're a part, but the simple magic of everyday life—magic things like flowers, fancily woven spider webs, and like this magnificent elephant."

"It's a shame," Gibbons said, "but most people take everyday magic for granted and fail to notice it. And in some ways, it's more spectacular than the hidden magic of things like living toys."

"Burl," Patch said, putting one paw on his friend's shoulder, "if I had the power to make it happen, I would transform you into an elephant as real and big as this one and send you to the veldt to fulfill your dreams. I see now why you'd long for such a life."

Skippy put one paw on Burl's other shoulder and said, "I'll make no more jokes about your hose nose or about your ears."

"Thank you, Skippy," Burl said softly.

"But I'll still snap your suspenders now and then," Skippy said. "And I'll still make mouse jokes."

"Fair enough," Burl said.

After a moment of silence during which they all stared up at the proud giant, Amos said, "I'm reminded of a poem by Rupert Toon—"

Even the elephant seemed to join in the groaning.

2.

The black bus rocketed through the stormy night. Its progress was not even slightly hindered by the treacherously slick highway.

By the time they crossed the city limits, the snow-pale driver, dressed all in black, had not said one word to Nick Jagg. Once in a while he raised his ice-

gray eyes to a mirror that gave him a view of the interior of the bus. In that mirror he studied Jagg for so long that it seemed he could not be in control of the vehicle. But he never spoke.

Sometimes Jagg returned the driver's strange stare, but mostly he just turned his head to the side and looked out at the silvery sleet whipping through the darkness.

As they crossed the city limits, a peculiar change occurred in that bus window in front of Jagg's face. His own vague reflection rippled, shimmered, and vanished. It was replaced by another face: smoky, sullen red eyes; a twisted mouth filled with exceedingly sharp teeth; the other features, though shadowy and indistinct, were clearly not human. It was the same face he had seen in the bathroom mirror at the bus station.

"Not long now," the Dark One said. "Soon your destiny will be fulfilled. Soon you will buy the toy factory, and you will be the new toymaker."

Jagg smiled.

Most criminal types like Jagg would have been thinking about all that lovely money in the suitcase. They would have been scheming to keep it even though it was the Devil's own money and would not be easily stolen. There was enough cash to allow him to live in luxury for a long time. But Jagg had no such thoughts. He did not care about the money. He dreamed only about making toys that would harm little children, toys that would bring misery into countless lives. Those mean-spirited thoughts excited him.

To the red-eyed face in the bus window, Nick Jagg said, "Thank you for giving me this wonderful opportunity."

The face smiled back at him.

Although it was only a reflection in the glass, he smelled its terrible, sulfurous breath.

Then it disappeared, and his own dim reflection replaced that of his demonic patron.

3.

Rex led Lizzie, Gear, and Jack Weasel along a twisty walkway in the park, under the wind-rattled branches of barren trees.

"They're here," Rex said. "Somewhere in the park. Not far away now. We'll get them this time."

"Break them," Gear said.

"Burn them," Lizzie said.

"Chew them up with my sharp wooden teeth," Jack said.

Suddenly Stinger swooped out of the sleet-slashed night and hovered in front of them. He had recovered from his collision with the bookshop sign, though both of his antennae were somewhat bent. "Thissss way," the bee said excitedly. "I've sssseen them. Thissss way to the Oddkinsssss."

4.

Victor Bodkins finally took shelter from the storm in an all-night coffeeshop.

The restaurant was warm and cozy. The air smelled of coffee, frying eggs, and bacon. The counter, stools, tables, and blue vinyl booths were clean, and everything gleamed.

When Victor first walked in, the two waitresses stared at him, as if debating whether to tell him that they did not serve bums like him. But then he took off his filthy, torn raincoat. His other clothes—except for his shoes and trousers—were still reasonably presentable, so the waitresses did not ask him to leave.

The place was not busy tonight. Other than Victor, the only customers were uniformed police officers who came and went in pairs.

He sat alone in a booth by the front windows, which were mostly steamed over. Like a witch's hooked fingernails, sleet ticked against the glass.

Victor ordered a piece of apple pie and coffee.

Using a paper napkin, he wiped a patch of condensation from the window and stared out at the wet and gloomy street, trying to make sense of what had happened to him this night.

He ate only two bites of the pie. It stuck in his throat and was hard to swallow. But the coffee went down easily.

He was nearly finished with his second cup of coffee when he saw the black bus pull up at the curb on the far side of the avenue. He had never seen a totally black bus before. For a moment he thought his eyes were deceiving him. He used another napkin to wipe at the steamed window again, clearing a larger portion of the glass.

No, it was definitely a black bus.

Completely, utterly black.

A very strange bus.

5.

Amos and the other Oddkins had reluctantly left the elephant at the zoo and had made their way along a series of paths in search of an exit from the park. In a shallow glen, as they passed beneath the drooping boughs of ice-crusted evergreens, they heard Jack Weasel's thin, mad giggle. The jack-in-the-box's laughter had not come from close at hand; it echoed from farther back along the walkway or perhaps from another walkway altogether, an eerie sound that seemed to slither low across the cold ground just like the wispy tendrils of fog that curled and eddied on all sides.

"They've found us," Skippy said, skidding to a halt.

"No," Amos said, grabbing the rabbit's arm and pulling him along. "They're nearby, but they haven't found us yet. However, they will find us if we don't hurry. We'll have to run as fast as we can . . . though I don't think we can outrun Jack Weasel."

"Think positive," Butterscotch said, trotting at Amos's side. "Maybe Weasel will have a flat tire."

"Not with his steel wheels," Amos said.

"Maybe he'll run head-on into a lamppost and knock himself senseless," Patch said.

"Maybe he'll take a shortcut through the elephant pen and get squished," Burl said.

"Maybe aliens will land in a flying saucer and kidnap him," said Skippy.

"We can't expect to be saved by an accident or by aliens," Amos said. "The only way we'll be saved is if we save ourselves. Good people can't triumph over bad people just by *being* good; they have to act."

"He's right," Gibbons said, caning himself along as fast as he could. "History proves what Amos just said."

"Run fast," Amos repeated. "And stay under the trees or scurry along beneath the shrubbery as much as possible because the bee might be looking for us. It might be flying overhead, scanning the ground, so we've not only got to move fast but stay out of sight as well."

"The bee must've bashed itself to pieces when it hit the sign," Patch said.

"We don't know for sure," Amos said. "We've got to figure that the bee is still around."

"Well, you're sure a cheerful sort," Skippy said sourly.

"You can't expect Amos always to be in a sunny mood at this time of the year," Burl said. "He's meant to be hibernating now, after all. He should be snoozing in a cave, dreaming of honey and wild berries. So of course he's cranky."

"I'm not cranky," Amos said as he hurried them along the evergreen-shrouded walkway. "Just worried and careful."

"Cranky," Burl insisted.

"Am not."

"Cranky," Patch agreed.

"Am not."

"Does Rupert Toon have anything to say about crankiness?" Skippy asked scornfully.

"*No!*" the other four Oddkins chorused as one.

"No time for Rupert Toon," Amos said as they reached the place where the sheltering pines stopped.

The walkway led across an open field where the bee, if cruising above, would spot them right away. Fortunately, a wide row of evergreen shrubs flanked one side of the walk, and they were able to continue in the shelter of those plants.

They had to crawl a lot because the shrubs grew low to the ground, providing little room to get under the branches. In some places they had to wriggle along on their bellies, and a couple of times Amos heard Patch moaning about the further deterioration in his appearance.

As they made their way to the edge of the park, they heard the distant giggle of Jack Weasel. Sometimes the jack-in-the-box sounded closer than at other times, as if he repeatedly passed nearby without sensing them. That was probably just a trick of the chilly, sleet-filled night air.

They heard a droning noise, too, which might have been a big plane passing over the city, high above the storm. Or it might have been a certain toy bee swooping low over the park.

"What Uncle Isaac should have done," Skippy whispered, "was make us twenty feet tall. We could have walked to Mrs. Shannon's place real fast, and no bad toys would have tried to stop us."

"It would be a little hard to keep people from seeing us if we were twenty feet tall, don't you think?" Amos whispered.

They crawled for a while as Skippy thought about that. At last he said, "Well, we could have tied long strings to ourselves and then, each time we ran into people, we could pretend to be giant animal balloons in some sort of parade."

At last they came to the end of the long row of bristly shrubbery and stepped onto a sidewalk flanked by tall stone pillars. Beyond the pillars were a street, buildings, the city. They had reached the end of the park.

"Which way now?" Gibbons asked Amos.

Frowning, Amos looked left, right, and straight ahead.

The sleet began to cover them with ice again.

Along the avenue, traffic lights turned from red to green, though there was no traffic.

"Maybe it'd be better if a horse was leading us," Burl said. "No offense meant, Amos, but they say horses have a good sense of direction."

"A homing pigeon would be even better," Patch said. "Homing pigeons have a terrific sense of direction."

"Of course, if Amos was a homing pigeon," Skippy said, "he'd have to have another name. Amos is a silly name for a pigeon."

"We could call him . . . Tweetie," Burl said.

"Or maybe Beaky," Skippy said.

Patch said, "Or Featherface."

"Or Wingo."

"Or Birdie."

"Peter Pigeon," Burl said. "Yeah, I like the sound of that. Let's call him Peter Pigeon."

"He's still a bear," Gibbons reminded them.

"Oh, yeah," Burl said.

"Too bad," Skippy said. "I don't think bears have any sense of direction at all."

"Give Amos a chance," Butterscotch said.

"That way," Amos said, pointing straight across the street. "That's the way to Mrs. Shannon's toy shop." He led them across the sidewalk, through six-inch-deep icy slop in the gutter, and out onto the deserted avenue.

They were halfway to the other side of the broad street when they heard a cry behind them. Turning, they saw Rex and the other bad toys coming out of the park.

A man got off the black bus and came straight to the coffeeshop. He put his suitcase on the floor at the counter, sat on a stool, and ordered coffee.

When Victor Bodkins looked back at the street, the black bus was gone. He had never heard its engine start up. It seemed to have drifted away on the storm wind.

To Victor, the stranger looked like a hard, perhaps dangerous man. He thought he might be overreacting. But when he looked at the two policemen in the coffeeshop, he saw they were studying the new arrival with interest and suspicion.

Several times, the stranger glanced at Victor, and Victor always quickly looked down at his unfinished pie or out at the night.

Eventually the policemen left.

Only Victor, the stranger, the two waitresses, and the short-order cook remained. After a moment the hard-looking man put money on the counter to pay for his coffee, got off his stool, and picked up his suitcase. Surprisingly, the guy came straight to Victor and sat across the table from him.

"I believe you have a toy factory for sale?" the man said.

Victor was startled.

"Am I right? A toy factory?"

"Why . . . yes . . . but who are you?" Victor asked.

"I want to buy your factory."

Victor was confused. "Where did you come from? How do you know who I am?"

"My name's Nick Jagg."

The stranger lifted his suitcase onto the table, then quickly looked around the restaurant to be sure they weren't being watched. They were still the only two customers. The waitresses and the short-order cook were gathered at the counter, at the far end of the restaurant, involved in their own conversation.

Opening the suitcase, Jagg said, "I'll pay cash for the factory if you'll sell it now. Right now."

Victor stared in shock and disbelief at the tightly banded stacks of hundred-dollar bills that filled the suitcase. "But . . . th-th-there must be a m-m-million dollars in there."

"More than two million."

Victor's head was filled with fevered thoughts of the investments that the money could buy. He began to calculate interest rates, stock and bond prices, and his mind overflowed with torrents of numbers. He began to breathe heavily and to shake with excitement. Making money, using that money to make more money, reinvesting the profits from the profits to make more profits—those were things that Victor Bodkins understood. He was not at ease with the idea that there could be such things as magic toys, but he was perfectly comfortable with money.

As he stared into the suitcase, he began to feel that the weird events of the earlier part of the night were all part of a spell of temporary insanity. He had gone a little crazy, but now he was all right again. There were no such things as living toys, no such thing as real magic at work in the world. But *money* was real, and he knew what to do with more than two million dollars.

"Will you sell me the factory?" Nick Jagg asked.

"It's a most generous offer," Victor said, finally looking up from the stacks of hundred-dollar bills and meeting Jagg's eyes.

Those eyes jolted and frightened him. They were so hard, so cold. Mean.

Staring into Jagg's disturbing eyes, Victor recalled the strange black bus. His mind turned from thoughts of money, and he realized again how odd it was that Jagg should know there was a toy factory for sale, even though Victor had not yet advertised or announced his desire to sell. It was odder still that Jagg should know precisely where to find Victor on this night of all nights.

"How did you find me?" Victor asked.

"I have my ways," Jagg said.

"And what *are* those ways?"

"A friend told me where to find you."

"What friend?" Victor demanded. "A friend of mine? But no one knew where I was tonight. Not even *I* knew where I was going until I got here. Besides . . . I'm not pleased to admit this . . . but I don't actually *have* any friends. Never had time to make any. Always too busy with my investments. Now who are you and how did you find me?"

Scowling, Jagg said, "Look at the cash, Victor. Money is your friend. Your best and truest friend. You don't need any other friend but money. Look at the cash and think about what you can do with it, and you won't be worried any more about who I am or how I found you."

There was something hypnotic in Jagg's voice, and Victor was unable to keep his gaze from lowering to the cash-filled suitcase. The sight of all that money made him breathless, and his thoughts became muddled.

"Be sensible, Victor. Sell the factory to me now."

The factory *was* a curse. Look what the place had done to Isaac: it had kept him a child all his life, an irresponsible child. And having inherited the place only this morning, Victor had been cursed by it, too: running like a madman through city streets in a sleet storm, searching for imaginary magical toys.

"Sell, Victor. Sell. Sell to me and take your money and live happily ever after."

"Well . . ."

"Sell, sell to me, sell the place and live happily ever after."

Torn between wanting the money and wanting to believe that Isaac had, somehow, created magical toys, Victor was in emotional turmoil. He was frightened of his inability to resist the money, but he was also afraid to look up into Jagg's hate-filled eyes, so he turned his deeply troubled gaze to the night. That was

when he heard the small, barely audible voice just beyond the window:

"Booga-booga-booga!"

Puzzled, leaning closer to the window, he saw the stuffed toys on the sidewalk, hurrying past the coffeeshop. The rabbit was running backward, shouting at something that was following him and his stuffed-toy friends.

"Booga-booga-booga!"

The rabbit, the elephant, the cavalier cat, and the other Oddkins vanished to the right.

Astonished, Victor pressed his face to the glass, flattening his nose almost painfully against the cold pane, trying to see more.

"Over two million dollars, Victor," said Nick Jagg with new urgency.

The Oddkins had gone. Victor could not get another glimpse of them, but suddenly he saw the marionettes and the robot and the jack-in-the-box to his left. They rushed past the front of the coffeeshop in pursuit of the Oddkins.

In his haste to get out of the booth, Victor bumped the suitcase, which fell to the floor, scattering packets of hundred-dollar bills.

The waitresses and the short-order cook looked up in surprise, and their eyes widened at the sight of the money.

"Wait!" Jagg said.

But Victor ran, not even bothering to put on his raincoat. He threw open the door of the coffeeshop and dashed into the wind and sleet.

The nasty toys that had attacked him in the woods were just turning the corner at the end of the block.

Victor sprinted after them, slipped, fell, got up, slipped again, but kept going.

7.

Amos knew they had to get off the streets. For one thing, they could not outrun their enemies forever; they had to hide and hope to throw the bad toys off their trail. For another thing, the longer they stayed on the streets, even in the lonely hours of the night and in the middle of this terrible ice storm, the more likely they were to reveal themselves accidentally to people who were never meant to see them.

In a dimly lighted alleyway between two tall buildings, Amos found a small window that opened into the basement of one of the immense structures. It was much too narrow to admit a man and only just large enough to admit an Oddkin. It was unlocked, and Amos directed his friends through it, into the dark room beyond.

Gibbons, Patch, Butterscotch, and Burl slipped inside.

But Skippy hesitated and said, "Let me wait for those nasties and give them one more booga."

"No."

"I'm sure they didn't hear me before. When they hear me giving them a booga, they'll be so scared they'll run away like those alley cats."

"These creatures aren't as easily scared as alley cats."

Before Skippy could protest, Amos grabbed the rabbit by the tail and the nape of the neck and threw him through the open window, into the cellar.

As Amos eased himself through the opening after Skippy, he saw Jack Weasel roll into the far end of the alleyway. Certain that he had been spotted, Amos dropped into the cellar and let the window fall shut behind him.

8.

One of the waitresses tried to pick up a bundle of hundred-dollar bills, but Jagg screamed at her and threatened her with such fury that she broke into tears and backed away.

"I was only trying to help," she said.

"Stay away from me, all of you, or you'll be sorry," Jagg said angrily.

He threw the last of the spilled money back into the suitcase, slammed the lid, latched it, and carried the fortune out into the night, in search of Victor Bodkins.

9.

They were in a department store. Amos led them out of the cellar onto the ground floor.

Security lights were aglow throughout the building. Those dim yellow bulbs illuminated some aisles and displays of merchandise but left other areas deep in shadow. Amos figured there would be a couple of security guards too. But it was a very large building, and there was little chance that they would accidentally stumble into the night watchmen. They scared themselves several times, however, by mistaking mannequins for real people.

The ground floor offered a thousand hiding places for six stuffed-toy animals. But Amos did not want to hide. He intended to climb to the third floor, then sneak out by way of the back stairs or a freight elevator, leaving the marionette and its vicious cronies to search through the place for the rest of the night.

They wandered around the ground level before going upstairs because, initially, their soggy feet left wet footprints on the marble floor. When they were no longer leaving a trail, they went to the stilled escalators and ascended with considerable effort.

By then, they had dried out a little. Except for Butterscotch's injured foot and Patch's missing eye, they did not look in too sad a state, for the rain and sleet had washed off the worst of the mud that they had slogged through in the early part of their journey.

Patch even dared to look at himself in a couple of the mirrored pillars that they passed. "Battered," he said self-critically, "but with a certain style, a certain tattered charm."

The vast third floor was divided among the sporting-goods, home-entertainment, and toy departments. To pause and discuss their next move, Amos and his companions gathered in an aisle between towering displays of television sets and video-cassette recorders.

Turning slowly around, staring up at all the blank TV screens, Skippy said, "Someday, wouldn't it be nice to come in here while the store is open, look around at all these sets tuned to the same channel, and see my face on every tube? Skippy the Funny Bunny, superstar!" He sighed. "Oh, what a lovely dream."

"Sounds like a nightmare to me," Patch said.

"Nightmare," Burl agreed.

Gibbons nodded. "Nightmare."

"I didn't ask for a *vote*," Skippy said.

Looking back the way they had come, Butterscotch said, "Did I just hear something?"

They tensed and fell silent.

To Amos, the deserted department store seemed perfectly quiet. But spooky. Definitely spooky.

"Well . . . I guess I imagined it," Butterscotch said. But now she whispered— and she did not relax.

"What do we do next?" Burl asked.

"We find a set of back stairs or some other way out of the building," Amos said. "Then on to Mrs. Shannon's place."

"How far do we still have to go?" Patch asked.

"Not far," Amos said. "Maybe six or eight blocks."

"I'll bet it's miles," Skippy said wearily. "Hundreds and hundreds of miles."

"Only a few blocks," Amos insisted.

"How do you know?" Skippy asked.

"I . . . just know. It's a . . . hunch."

"Do bears have hunches?" Burl asked doubtfully.

"Bears have nice round bellies," Patch said.

"And bears have cute furry ears," Gibbons said.

"And bears have shiny black noses," said Butterscotch.

"And bears have four big paws," Burl said.

"But bears don't have hunches," Skippy said.

"Well, this bear does," Amos said. "And if you don't want to believe me, then I'll have to tell you what Rupert Toon said about bears and their hunches."

"We believe you," the other five Oddkins chorused.

"All right," Amos said. "Now, from here we'll go—"

Stepping out from between two console-model television sets and interrupting Amos, Rex said, "Hello, soft-bellied ones."

Jack Weasel wheeled into the aisle, grabbed Butterscotch's right ear, and spun in a circle, dragging her around with him, as if trying to tear the ear off her head.

Amos took a step toward Butterscotch, intending to help her, as did Burl. But Rex slashed out with his stiletto-tipped cane, and the blade flashed in the dim light, and Burl's right ear was lopped off.

"Oh, my!" the elephant said. "Look at that. My head's going to tilt to one side from now on. No good. No good at all."

"Let me even things up for you," Rex said, grinning and advancing with his cane at the ready.

"Well, sir," Burl said, backing away, "I suppose I can live with a bit of a tilt."

Having drawn his own sword, Patch stepped forward and said, "You've met your match now, you wooden-headed varlet!"

With a whoosh-whoosh-whoosh of cutting air, Rex made several passes with his swordlike cane, slicing Patch's rubber sword into five pieces and leaving the startled cat with only the rubber haft in his hand.

"You need more than play swords and good intentions to rid the world of *my* kind," Rex told Patch. "You can't just wish us away or count on your goodness to protect you."

The female marionette appeared, waving the magically red-hot plastic cigarette, trying to burn someone with it. All of the Oddkins who were not fending off Rex and Jack Weasel were forced to leap and scurry out of her way.

Amos felt a hand on his shoulder. Whirling around, he found himself face to face with the yellow-eyed robot.

"Break, rip, tear," the robot said.

"You seem to have a limited vocabulary," Amos said. He threw himself against the robot instead of trying to scramble away from it. At the same time he dropped to his knees and heaved the metal man into the air. The robot went over Amos's shoulders and crashed to the floor behind him.

Scrambling up, Amos saw that the robot was not injured and was clanking to its feet to continue the battle.

Only the bee had not appeared, and Amos looked worriedly up at the department-store ceiling, wondering from which direction the nasty insect would dive at them.

Laughing hysterically, Jack Weasel waved one of Butterscotch's ears in the air. "Let's dismantle the doggy. Let's take the doggy apart piece by piece!''

Burl and Patch were still dodging Rex's flashing blade.

Skippy was running in circles around the female marionette, shouting ''booga-booga-booga,'' waving his arms in what he seemed to think was a frightening manner, and making horrible faces in hopes of scaring her. And all the while he was trying to avoid being set afire by her cigarette.

Meanwhile, poor old Gibbons was trying to avoid Skippy, who twice collided with the elderly scholar and knocked him down.

This is bad, Amos thought. *They're going to destroy us in a few more minutes.*

''You're making me angry!'' Burl shouted at Rex, as he dodged the marionette's blade. ''And the last thing anyone wants to do is make an elephant angry.''

Amos rushed up behind Jack Weasel, grabbed the bottom of the mad creature's box, tilted it off its wheels, and gave it a shove. The jack-in-the-box slid along the aisle on his side, wheels spinning in the air, arms waving, screeching furiously. He crashed into the robot, and both of them crashed into Rex, leaving only the other marionette on her feet.

''Run!'' Amos cried to his friends. ''Run, run!''

They ran, too, fast as their stumpy, stuffed legs would carry them, along the aisle between the television sets and the video-cassette recorders.

For a moment Amos thought that all of his friends had escaped. But at a turn in the aisle, he glanced back and saw that the fallen robot had reached out with one steel hand and had seized Skippy by the ankle. The rabbit was held fast, unable to tear himself free.

Rex was getting to his feet, and Jack Weasel was struggling to put himself onto his wheels again.

''Oh, no,'' Butterscotch said. ''They've got Skippy. They've got poor Skippy.''

''We have to save him,'' Patch said.

''No,'' Amos said firmly. ''If we go back now, they'll only destroy all of us.

Then there will be no one to get through to Mrs. Shannon and tell her that she's been chosen as the new toymaker.''

''But we can't abandon Skippy,'' Burl said. ''I'll admit that his jokes aren't always funny, and sometimes he can be irritating, and he's too much of a wiseguy for his own good, but we still can't abandon him. He's our *friend*.''

Patch started back the way they had come.

''No!'' Amos said fiercely enough to stop the cat.

''Amos is right,'' Gibbons said. ''If we go back now, we'll be caught. But we don't have to abandon Skippy. We just have to retreat, regroup, find things we can use as weapons, then return to rescue him. But we can't go back until we're armed.''

Rex was standing again. The robot was on its knees and rising. In seconds, Jack Weasel would be back on his wheels.

''Let's get out of here,'' Amos said urgently.

The bear ran. His friends followed him out of the displays of home-entertainment equipment and into the enormous toy department at the south end of the third floor.

10.

Stinger buzzed through the sleet and wind, periodically shaking off the ice that formed on his wings. He circled the department store, keeping a watch on all sides. If he saw the Oddkins slipping out of the building, he would extend his stinger to three times its normal length, dive-bomb them, and tear the stuffing out of their soft cloth bodies.

He loved the night.

He loved the storm.

He loved his stinger.

11

"Bring the cotton-tailed wimp," Rex said. He stalked to the north end of the third floor, to the sporting-goods department.

"Wimp?" Skippy said in a voice touched by both fear and anger.

"Soft-bellied wimp," Jack Weasel said, rolling at Rex's side and favoring Skippy with an insane grin.

Gear clanked along at Rex's other side, holding Skippy tightly by the ears, half carrying and half dragging his captive.

Skippy said, "I'll have you know that I faced down a mongrel dog tonight. And stood bravely in the very shadow of a *real* elephant. And chased off some tough alley cats."

"I'm so impressed," Rex said with a mean laugh. "Oh, I'm so impressed, rabbit."

"So impressed," Jack Weasel echoed, then giggled.

"Do you think you could stand bravely, unflinchingly while I burned some holes in you with my cigarette?" Lizzie asked, waving the red-hot cylinder in the rabbit's face.

"Eeep! Get that away from me!" Skippy said. "If you burn me, I'll . . . I'll . . ."

"You'll what?" Lizzie asked. "Cry?"

"No!" Skippy said. "I'll just . . . go berserk! Yeah, that's what I'll do. I'll go berserk, and I won't be responsible for what'll happen then."

"Look at me," Rex said, pretending fear. "Oh, I'm scared so

bad, I'm shaking. A berserk rabbit. Oh, how terrible. Oh, how very fearsome you must be when you're in a rage."

Dangling by his ears from Gear's hand, trying to keep his feet on the floor but frequently being pulled into the air, Skippy said, "You bet. When I go berserk, I'm dangerous. Why, I might tear you all limb from limb—or wheel from wheel. When I'm through with you, you'll all be nothing but splinters and bits of twisted metal. Oh, it'll be just horrible. It makes me sick to think about it. But I can't help myself. When I go berserk, I have no control, none, I'm just a wild, dangerous maniac. Please don't anger me and make me harm you. Please don't."

The cruel laughter of the Charon toys echoed along the aisle.

"Well," Skippy said, "it was worth a try."

They stopped at last in front of a polished oak display case filled with rifles and shotguns.

Gear lifted Skippy off the floor again, and Rex put the sharp blade of his cane against the rabbit's throat. As Jack Weasel and Lizzie gathered around to watch, Rex said, "You know what happens next, you silly rabbit?"

Skippy swallowed hard. "Maybe you have a change of heart, take pity on me, let me go, and that's the end of it."

"No," Rex said. "That's not what happens next."

Skippy said, "Wait, give me another chance! Let's see . . . maybe what will happen next is that I'll think of a good joke, and you'll realize what a great Funny Bunny I am, and you'll spare me because I amuse you."

"I don't like jokes," Rex said.

"Juggling? I can juggle."

"I hate jugglers."

"Bird calls? I can whistle bird calls."

"I hate the pleasant, musical voices of birds. I prefer the harsh, ugly cry of a vulture."

"Oh, well, then maybe a herd of talking turnips will suddenly walk through the store, and you'll be so amazed by talking turnips that you'll forget all about me."

Rex blinked. "Are you crazy, rabbit? Do you really think that a herd of talking turnips might walk through here?"

Rolling his eyes to try to see the sharp blade at his throat, swallowing hard again, Skippy said, "I've got to have something to hope for, you know. I can't just give up."

"But talking turnips?"

"Well, maybe it'll be tap-dancing grapefruits," Skippy said.

Rex snarled as if he were a dog. "You're a totally crazy rabbit. Bah! I'll *tell* you what's going to happen next, you lop-eared fool." He pressed the blade harder against Skippy's throat. "We're going to lure and trap your soft-bellied friends. I'm not going to cut you up right away because, unhurt, you're good bait."

"Bait," Gear repeated in his icy voice.

"Bait," Jack Weasel said, and laughed shrilly.

"Bait?" Skippy said.

"Bait for your friends," Rex said. "No need for me and my crew to go running after them. I know their kind. Good-hearted fools, well-meaning simpletons. They can't abandon you. They're full of such nonsensical ideas as honor, duty, responsibility, and friendship. Oh, they'll be back to rescue you, sure enough, and we'll be ready for them. Do you see these guns behind us?"

Skippy rolled his eyes toward the display case full of deadly looking weapons.

Rex said, "They also sell ammunition here. We'll take down a couple of the guns, load them, and hide with them. When your friends come back to save you, we won't risk letting them slip through our fingers again. We'll wait until they walk right in front of the guns, then pull the triggers. We'll blow all the stuffing out of them."

"That's really nasty," Skippy said.

Rex grinned. "I love to be nasty."

"Me too!" Jack Weasel said.

"Nasty is so nice," said Lizzie.

"Guns are bad," Skippy said urgently.

"I like bad things," Rex said. "Gear, turn the rabbit around."

Still holding Skippy by the ears, Gear turned the rabbit.

Rex's blade went *snick*.

"Hey!" Skippy cried.

Rex had cut off the perfect powder-puff tail that had once graced Skippy's bottom.

"That," said the marionette, "is how quickly I will lop off your head when the time comes."

"How can I be a superstar without a cute tail to wiggle?" Skippy moaned. "Bugs Bunny has a cute tail. The white rabbit in *Alice in Wonderland* has a cute tail. All famous rabbits have cute tails."

"Yours wasn't that cute anyway," Rex said, tossing the tail aside.

"Listen, you sick puppet," Skippy said, "if you don't let me go, if you don't let my friends alone, I'll . . ."

"You'll what?" Rex asked, leaning close, his wooden nose almost touching Skippy's nose.

Gear shook Skippy by the ears.

Rex said, "Hmmmmm? What will you do, rabbit?"

"I hate to threaten something like this," Skippy said. "It's awfully cruel, I know. But if you don't behave, I'll just have to recite some Rupert Toon poetry. What do you think of that? Bet that has you shaking in your boots!"

"Who is Rupert Toon?" Rex asked.

"Just the worst poet who ever wrote a line, so bad he'll make you fall to your knees and beg for mercy."

Rex smiled wickedly. "Try me."

Skippy hesitated.

"What's wrong, rabbit?"

"I can't remember any of Toon's verse. I've forced myself to forget every line of it. But if I *could* remember, you'd be whimpering and begging for mercy."

"Bah!" Rex said. To Lizzie he said, "Come on. Help me get two of the shotguns out of this case."

12.

In the toy department, Amos was sitting in a battery-powered car designed for children more than twice his size. The car was sleek and snazzy: bright blue with red and yellow flames painted over the hood and along the sides; chrome wheels; an open top with a wide rollbar. Amos felt very sporty (for a bear), but he was also frightened and worried.

"It's easy," Gibbons said, using his cane to point to an illustration in the instruction booklet, which he had spread out on the black-and-white-tile floor.

With one paw on the steering wheel, Amos leaned far enough out of the car to peer down at the booklet. "Doesn't look easy to me. Looks like I could get into big trouble trying to steer this buggy around a department store."

"It's child's play," Gibbons assured him. "After all, this is a child's car, a *toy* car."

"A big toy," Amos protested.

"But still a toy. And if a child can handle it, so can you."

Butterscotch was standing on the hood of the car, looking at a bunch of stuffed-toy animals stacked between displays of Bug Man action figures and Sergeant Salvo dolls. "Amos, do you see that these poor creatures can't talk or move?" she asked.

Amos had seen the stuffed animals earlier and had recognized some of them from the funny pages of the newspapers he had read: Garfield the cat, Opus the penguin, Bill the cat, and others. To Butterscotch, he said, "Well, of course, they can't talk or move. They're only toys."

"But we're only toys," Butterscotch said, "yet we can talk and move."

"We're magic toys," Gibbons reminded her.

Butterscotch looked very sad. "Well, yes, I know that we're special, that we have a destiny to help children who are in need of special guidance. But I'd always thought that ordinary toys could at least move and talk a *little* bit."

"Not at all," Gibbons said.

"It seems so unfair," Butterscotch said, for she was a loving and compassionate dog who wanted everyone—and every stuffed thing—to share her pleasure in being alive.

Above the sports car, Patch and Burl were standing atop a pile of cartons. They were busily extracting a Galactic Hero Photon Burp Gun from the colorful cardboard box in which it was packed. The gun shot Ping-Pong balls, and according to the box it was the "terror of all aliens."

Amos did not like guns, partly because hunters used guns to shoot real bears. Of course *this* gun could not really harm anyone, but it made Amos nervous anyway.

The weapon was too large for one Oddkin, but perhaps Patch and Burl could carry it together.

"You'll hold the barrel steady," Burl said, "while I hold the stock of the gun and pull the trigger."

"No," Patch said, "I'll pull the trigger."

"I'll pull the trigger," Burl insisted.

"I will," Patch said.

"Let's not argue about this," Burl said, "because if we argue, you're liable to get squished."

"You shouldn't threaten to squish me," Patch said. "I'm your friend."

"Sorry," Burl said. "It would only be a friendly little squish."

"Amos," Gibbons said sternly, "pay attention to me, not to them. If we're to save Skippy, you absolutely must learn to drive this car."

"Do we really have a chance of saving him?" Amos asked, for he was weary and full of self-doubt. "An elderly scholar, a one-eared dog with a lame foot, a one-eared elephant, and a one-eyed cat—all led by a bear who likes poetry. Somehow, we don't seem like a very threatening group."

"A missing eye and a couple of missing ears don't mean anything," said Gibbons. "We're still the same stout-hearted group we were when we set out from the toy factory."

"Well . . ."

"We can do it," Gibbons said.

"How can you be so sure we can?"

"How can you be sure we *can't*?"

Amos sighed. "This won't be easy."

"Many things in life aren't easy."

"Yeah, I know. And a quest like this is always hard."

"That's right. But if a person has courage and determination, he or she can always do what's necessary."

"Why don't *you* drive the car?"

"I'll be driving the other one," Gibbons reminded him.

Amos sighed again.

"Now will you pay attention to this instruction booklet?" old Gibbons asked.

"Okeydoke."

13.

Gear stood in the center of the aisle where the camping equipment was sold, directly under one of the all-night security lamps. His metal skin shone brightly. He held Skippy by the ears and waited patiently for something to happen.

Hidden inside a tent in a camping-equipment display, Lizzie waited to pull the trigger of a shotgun. The gun had been carefully propped on several boxes, lined up to cover part of the aisle to Skippy's left, and wedged in place with more boxes and a tightly rolled sleeping bag. Only the muzzle of the gun was visible where it poked out between the canvas flaps of the tent.

Half-concealed beside a pile of fishing gear, Jack Weasel manned another shotgun that the Charon toys had worked hard to put in place. That one had been propped in such a way that it covered part of the aisle to Skippy's right.

Rex was behind a snowmobile, lying on top of a third shotgun that covered the intersection where the main aisle met another. Only one corner of the marionette's top hat was visible.

Dangling by his ears from the robot's hand, Skippy said, "It won't work, you know. It won't work, you big bucket of bolts."

Gear said nothing.

"For one thing," Skippy said, "I'll bet none of you guys have used guns before. You don't know what you're doing."

Gear said nothing.

"For another thing," Skippy said, "my friends are too clever for you. Oh, yes, very clever. They'll run circles around your friends and won't let anyone get a clear shot at them."

Gear said nothing.

"Besides," Skippy said, "the moment I see them coming, I'll call out to them and warn them."

Gear clamped his other hand over Skippy's mouth.

"Mmmmphhh. Smmmphhh."

Gear said, "Dumb bunny."

14.

Buzz, buzz, buzz.

Outside, Stinger swooped around and around the department store, scanning the streets and alleys on all sides, looking for Oddkins.

He saw none.

But he did see two men in the deserted, winter-swept city below him, the first of whom seemed bewildered. It was the man they had attacked in the woods earlier in the night. He was wandering through the sleet storm without a coat. His suit was soaked. He must have been half-frozen, but he ran this way and that, frantically looking behind mailboxes and trash cans, peering into shadowy doorways, searching for something.

The second man moved slower than the first but in a straight line. He was coming down the same avenue, and he was carrying a big suitcase.

The moment Stinger saw the man with the suitcase, the bee became excited. He soared high into the stormy night, did a couple of wild barrel rolls, and swooped in a figure eight.

The night itself seemed to speak to Stinger in a faint, eerie voice, and it said, "Here comes your new master, the new toymaker, here he comes, a man who hates children but who loves your kind and will make more of you."

"We're going to win," Stinger said. "Yesssss, yesssss, we're sssssurely going to win thisssss war."

Buzz, buzz, buzz.

15.

Rex heard a soft humming noise. Before he realized what was happening, the bear swept past him in a battery-powered sports car.

The one-eyed, cavalier cat was sitting beside the bear, in the second bucket seat, holding the stocks of a strange-looking gun. The elephant was perched precari-

ously on the hood of the car, directly in front of the cat, and he was both holding and aiming the barrel of that same weapon.

Lying atop the well-braced shotgun, Rex reached down with both hands and pulled the trigger. But the sports car was too fast. The blast missed the back end of the car and tore apart a display of thermos bottles and ice chests on the other side of the aisle. The power of the shot knocked the gun off its props and also sent Rex tumbling backwards as if he were a just a scrap of gauze caught in a strong wind.

The first car was past Lizzie before she realized what was happening. The second car, driven by the old Oddkin, with the dog in the passenger's seat, hummed along close behind the first, so she took a shot at that one.

The recoil threw both her and the gun through the back of the tent, which collapsed. Screeching angrily, she struggled to claw her way out of the rumpled canvas.

Jack Weasel saw that some of the pellets from Lizzie's shot did indeed hit the second car, but not enough of them to destroy either the dog or the old geezer. The car had holes in it, but it was still running.

The first car sped past Gear and the rabbit.

Jack was ready to pull the trigger the moment the Oddkins were in his line of fire. But suddenly they turned off the aisle and drove into the display of fishing gear where he was hidden. Unable to shoot them when they failed to drive through his sights, Weasel turned away from the gun and rolled forward to meet the car. He hoped to reach out and pull the elephant off the hood as they sped by.

But then he saw that the elephant and the cat were operating a strange gun of their own, and an instant later—

Ponk-ponk-ponk!

—Weasel was hit in the face by three white plastic balls.

He didn't seem to be hurt, but he was badly startled. He dropped back into his box and slammed the lid over his head, deciding to hide in there for a moment until he could figure out whether the gun they were using was dangerous.

The first car sped out of the display of fishing equipment and braked close to Gear, fishtailing slightly.

The elephant lined up the space-age weapon, and the cat pulled the trigger, and Gear was hit in the face—

Ponk-ponk-ponk-ponk!

—by four plastic balls.

The forceful impact of the balls made him totter on his clumsy metal feet, but he was unhurt.

Ponk-ponk-ponk!

The elephant shouted, "Take that, tin-can head!"

Unhurt but angered by these pesky, soft-bellied creatures, Gear dropped the rabbit and lunged toward the car, both metal hands outstretched. He intended to grab the car and rock it until he rocked them out; then he would pound on them with his metal fists until he had flattened every one of them into shapeless wads of cloth and cotton stuffing.

The moment the robot let go of Skippy, Gibbons drove the second car past Amos's vehicle and braked beside the rabbit.

"Climb on!" Butterscotch shouted from the passenger's seat.

For once the rabbit did not pause to make a joke. He hopped right onto the back of the car, holding tight to the rollbar with both forepaws. "Let's get out of here!"

Ponk! Patch and Burl fired their last Ping-Pong ball.

The robot put one hand on the car.

Amos took his foot off the brake and tramped on the accelerator, but the robot's one-handed grip was strong enough to hold them. The tires spun on the tile floor, but the car would not move.

Patch said, "Hey, big fella, wouldn't you like to own the most destructive weapon in the known universe? Wouldn't you like to wipe out whole cities and blow apart mountains?"

The robot had been reaching for Patch's head with its free hand. Now it hesitated, and its yellow eyes flashed bright. "Sure."

"Wouldn't you like to have everyone fear you, even Rex, and wouldn't you like to be able to crush *anyone* who got in your way?"

"Crush, tear, rip, break," said the robot.

"Crush, tear, rip, break," Patch said encouragingly.

"Squish too," said Burl.

"Squish, crush, tear, rip, break," the robot said.

"Then this is exactly what you need," Patch said, handing the Galactic Hero Photon Burp Gun—"terror of all aliens"—to the robot.

Confused, the evil creature let go of the car and accepted the empty gun.

"Go, Amos!" Burl and Patch shouted.

Amos jammed his paw on the accelerator, and they got out of there before the robot could drop the gun and grab the car again.

With Skippy hanging on to the top of the car, Gibbons wheeled toward the escape route they had planned to use. But to his surprise, the female marionette stumbled out of the wreckage of a display of camping equipment and stepped in front of them. He had no time to brake or avoid her. She looked up, surprised, and Gibbons hit her.

The marionette disintegrated. Her wooden head popped off. Her left leg broke free of her body and flew to the right, and her right leg flew to the left. One arm spun high into the air, and the other arm fell into the car with Gibbons and Butterscotch.

It was the arm with the cigarette holder, and it was still full of evil life. It clawed its way up from the seat and poked the red-hot cigarette at Gibbons's head, setting his white hair on fire.

Snarling, Butterscotch grabbed hold of the arm with her mouth. She stood on the seat, put two paws on the door, leaned with her head outside the car, and dropped the evil limb into the aisle even as it tried to turn the glowing cigarette on her.

Gibbons let go of the wheel to beat at his blazing hair with both hands. The car careened back and forth.

Just as he put out the fire, he saw a familiar bright red box rolling toward them. He did not fully recognize it until the lid opened and Jack Weasel popped out to see where he was going.

"Awk!" Weasel shouted when he saw the car bearing down on him.

Gibbons tramped on the brake.

They collided.

Weasel did not disintegrate as the marionette had done, but he was knocked on his side.

The instant the car stopped, Skippy hopped off and ran to a pile of camping equipment.

"Skippy, get back here!" Butterscotch cried.

But Skippy had seen something useful and had formed a plan to get rid of Jack Weasel once and for all. The rabbit returned in seconds with a pair of bungee cords that had been part of the ruined camping display. As Weasel pulled himself back onto his wheels, Skippy slammed the lid on the red box and belly-flopped on top of it, holding it shut. From within, Weasel tried to force the lid up, but Skippy held fast and began trying to wrap one of the bungee cords around the box.

Gibbons climbed out of the car and hurried to Skippy's aid. Together, they hooked one cord from front to back around the box and wrapped the other around from the opposing direction.

Inside, Jack Weasel screamed and pounded furiously on the walls of his portable home—which had abruptly become his prison.

"Follow me in the car," Skippy said.

"Where are you going?" Gibbons asked.

"To the escalators," Skippy said.

"Excellent idea. Oh, what happened to your tail?"

"Evolution," Skippy said.

Confused by that answer, Gibbons hobbled to the car, got behind the wheel and followed Skippy as the rabbit raced down one aisle and then another, pushing the jack-in-the-box ahead of him. At the top of the down escalator, where a security light glowed particularly bright, Skippy gave the red box one last shove.

Jack Weasel went tumbling down that long flight of grooved, metal stairs.

Amos pulled up in the other car with Burl and Patch. Everyone gathered at the head of the escalator to look down on the splintered debris that had once been Jack Weasel.

"He should have taken the elevator," Skippy said.

Everyone laughed, and Amos said, "Skippy, that was a *good* joke!"

Skippy beamed happily.

At that very moment alarms began to ring throughout the huge department store.

"The night watchmen," Gibbons said. "They must've heard the shotguns. The police will be here soon."

"I like adventure as much as the next cat," Patch said, "but I'm beginning to think this is too much adventure."

In the aisle down which Amos and Gibbons had driven, Rex and the robot were hurrying toward the Oddkins.

"Quickly," Amos said. "Let's climb the next escalator to the fourth floor."

16.

Half-frozen and becoming depressed again, Victor was passing by the front entrance of the department store when the alarms began to ring inside.

Somehow he knew at once that the commotion had nothing to do with ordinary burglars but was related to the toys he'd been pursuing all night. Slipping on the sleet-filmed sidewalk, he hurried as best he could to the main doors. They were locked, of course. He put his face to the glass and peered into the store, but he could see nothing out of the ordinary.

Sleet crunched and crackled beneath his feet as he made his way along the side of the building, seeking a way inside. He had gone only ten or twelve steps when he heard a peculiar buzzing noise mixed with the keening of the wind.

When he looked up, he saw something small and fast sail through the night twenty feet overhead.

Even if he'd not had a brief glimpse of its yellow-and-black-striped body, even if he had not seen its two hateful red eyes turned down at him as it passed, he would have known it was the toy bee. He squinted into the slashing sleet and saw the creature swoop around the north corner of the building, out of sight.

It's patrolling the perimeter, he thought. *So something* is *going on inside.*

As Victor hurried toward the north corner of the building, he heard Nick Jagg shouting behind him:

"Bodkins! Wait! The money, Bodkins! It's a lot of money!"

17.

At the head of the escalator on the fourth floor, the Oddkins found the housewares department to the left and the gourmet food department to the right.

Below, Rex was nowhere to be seen, but Gear was a third of the way up the stilled metal steps.

Raising his voice to be heard above the noisy alarms, Amos said, "Find things to throw down at him."

Gibbons and Patch hurried to the gourmet department and returned with two cans of imported hazelnut purée and two of tender white asparagus spears. They threw those missiles at Gear.

The robot dodged the cans and continued upward.

Amos plucked a four-slice toaster from a display, lugged it to the escalator, and sent it crashing down toward the robot. It bounced noisily off several risers but stopped one step short of Gear, leaving him unharmed.

"Where's Rex?" Skippy asked worriedly.

"I don't know," Amos said. "I wish I did."

"And the bee?"

"Haven't seen him either."

"I'll bet they're sneaking up on us."

"Maybe," Amos said.

"And in disguise," Skippy said uneasily.

"What disguise?"

"Who knows. Could be disguised as anything, anyone . . ."

Burl trotted up with a tin of Belgian butter cookies.

"Could be disguised as Burl!" Skippy said, stepping back from the elephant in fear.

Burl said, "Huh?"

Skippy said, "Who are you?"

Burl looked puzzled. "I'm me."

"Are you really?" Skippy asked suspiciously.

Blinking at Amos, Burl said, "Maybe Skippy's smarts were in his tail. He seems dumber now that Rex cut it off."

Looking aghast at Amos, Skippy said, "How can I be sure that even you are really who you seem to be?"

"And how can we be sure that you're really Skippy?" Amos asked.

Burl stared at them a moment, then shrugged. "Somehow, both Skippy *and* you must've got dumber when Rex cut his tail off." He looked down the escalator at Gear. "He's a stubborn hunk of scrap iron, isn't he?" Burl threw the tin of butter cookies at the robot.

Gear crouched, hiding behind a riser as much as possible. The cookie tin bounced off the top of his head, but he rose immediately, unscathed, his yellow eyes glowing as brightly as ever.

Amos grabbed another toaster and threw it, and Patch tossed two small jars of caviar, which broke and splattered Gear with bits of glass and fish eggs. Gibbons threw jars of gourmet ice-cream topping—chocolate fudge, caramel, brandy rum sauce—and Burl heaved down two more tins of cookies, one of which burst open. Butterscotch used her nose to roll a couple of vases down the escalator, adding to the litter of broken glass. Though casting suspicious looks at each of his friends, fearing one of them was Rex in disguise, Skippy joined in the barrage, throwing a cheese grater, a potato peeler, two cannisters of teabags, and a pair of brass candlesticks.

The escalator was a mess. It oozed and dripped a disgusting variety of foodstuffs out of which poked metal and glass debris of all sizes and shapes.

But Gear was still climbing upward. He had been hit a couple of times, but nothing had seriously damaged him.

"Time for the heavy artillery," Amos said. "Come on."

He led the other Oddkins to a wheeled tea cart that was stacked with English china. By joining forces, they were able to move the heavy cart to the head of the escalator and tip it over the edge.

Below, the robot looked up at the approaching avalanche and said, "Bad for Gear."

Then the tea cart and dishes hit the robot and carried him all the way to the bottom of the escalator, where he was pinned under the rubble and so badly broken that the yellow light in his eyes flickered and went out.

18.

Victor Bodkins heard sirens in the distance and figured the cops were coming in answer to the department store alarms. He ran along the north side of the building and turned the corner into an alleyway behind it.

He was aware that Jagg was following, slowed by the suitcase full of hundred-dollar bills, but he did not care. The only thing he cared about right now was finding those toys.

As he sloshed through the icy puddles in the alley, a fire door in the back of the department store opened forty feet ahead of him. Several stuffed-toy animals toppled out into the night. They had been standing on one another's shoulders in order to reach the release bar that operated the door, and when the door gave way they had pitched outward. Those toward the top of the balancing act fell the farthest, splashing onto the puddled pavement.

The bear and the elephant, evidently having formed the base of the pyramid, stumbled out with the rabbit balanced precariously on their shoulders.

"Eeep!" the rabbit cried.

The bear and the elephant nearly fell over the old Dickensian creature, who had fallen out ahead of them.

Wobbling atop the bear's and the elephant's shoulders, the rabbit again cried, "Eeep!"

The bear and the elephant staggered to the left.

"Eeep!"

They staggered to the right.

"Eeep!"

They nearly fell over the dog and then actually did fall over the cavalier cat.

"Eeeeeeeeep!"

Pitched off the shoulders of his companions, the rabbit landed face down in a sleet-skinned puddle, and came up spluttering. "You guys would never have made it in vaudeville!"

Victor Bodkins stared at the small creatures with surprise, wonder, and delight.

They suddenly noticed him and froze.

After a moment the bear said, "Well, at least it's the *same* adult."

Before Victor could even try to figure what that meant, he saw the tuxedo-clad marionette leap out from behind a garbage dumpster and slash at the elephant with a sword-tipped cane. The elephant's trunk was lopped off.

"No!" the bear cried, and with great courage he charged the marionette.

The bee plummeted straight out of the sky and hit the bear so hard that they both went tumbling backward. The bee's stinger was enormous and sharp, and it pierced the teddy bear's chest, poking out of the middle of poor bruin's back, completely skewering him. Wriggling, the bee pulled free of his victim and zoomed up into the night again.

During the bee's attack, the marionette had been moving in. As the bear began to sit up, the marionette pounced on him. The blade flickered in the dim light of the alley's nearest security lamp. Cotton stuffings were torn from the bear and were thrown all over the pavement.

"No!" the trunkless, one-eared elephant cried.

The cat and the rabbit threw themselves at the marionette, but the evil puppet pitched them away with supernatural strength and cut the bear again.

The dog leaped upon the marionette and tried to sink her soft teeth into its hard neck.

It heaved free of her.

Then all five of the bear's companions joined the fray. Their small angry voices filled the alleyway in spite of the growing clamor of police sirens.

Victor rushed forward, hoping to separate the combatants and restrain the marionette.

The bee swooped down and hovered in front of Victor's face. Its long, wickedly sharp stinger pointed at his eyes. "Ssssstay out of thissss."

Victor halted. He was confused and frightened. But he was neither so confused nor so frightened that he was unable to act. Seeing the lid of a trash can lying at his feet, he bent and picked it up and swung it at the bee in one swift, smooth movement.

CLANG!

The bee was thrown into the wall of the building. It struck hard and fell to the pavement.

Before it could pop up and fly away, Victor stamped on it once, twice, again and again, until he felt it crack into pieces under his shoe.

Turning to the Oddkins again, he saw that the elephant and the cat were using another trash-can lid as a shield and were driving the marionette backward, away from the savaged teddy bear. Behind the marionette, the old-looking Oddkin, the rabbit, and the dog had worked a manhole cover out of its spot in the pavement. They were evidently hoping that the marionette could be tricked into stepping backward into the hole.

But the marionette turned, saw the trap, and laughed nastily. "I'm afraid I won't be that easy to dispose of, you soft-bellied fools. I'll rip the stuffing out of all of you, and that will be the end."

"No," Victor said. He ran forward and kicked the marionette straight into the manhole. It fell down into the storm drain with a furious cry of rage.

Victor slid the iron cover into place, trapping the malevolent creature below.

The Oddkins had gathered around the damaged teddy bear. They were sobbing. Victor had never before heard such a sad, sorry sound.

The sirens were nearer but still a couple of blocks away. In the city's icy streets, even the police could not travel as fast as they wanted.

Nick Jagg had come halfway along the alley with his suitcase full of money. "Victor . . ."

Victor ignored him. He joined the Oddkins, kneeling beside the teddy bear.

The ravaged bruin lay on his back, arms spread. His eyes were glassy buttons, and he looked as if he had never been alive. Most of the cotton stuffing had been torn out of him, leaving only the sagging, furry material that served as his skin.

"Amos," the elephant said. "Oh, Amos, Amos, please sit up and speak to us."

"Please," Skippy said. "Amos, please lead us."

But the bear did not move or speak.

"He's lost too much stuffing," Butterscotch said. "Poor, dear, noble Amos is gone."

Looking at each of the five living animals in turn, Victor said, "I don't know what you are or what you've set out to do tonight. I don't understand how you could be alive or how this bear, once having lived, could be dead. But wherever you need to go, I'll take you. Whatever you need, I'll get it for you. I want to help you. I think you are my Uncle Isaac's children, and I want to do anything I can for you. Please let me help."

"Take the money, you stupid fool," Jagg said, suddenly looming over them. He was a tall, shadowy, menacing figure. He had put the suitcase on the pavement. Now he popped the latches and opened the lid. Sleet tapped on the tightly banded hundred-dollar bills. "Take the money and go. You're up against powerful forces, the forces of Darkness, and there's no way you can win. Take the money."

"You were on the side of those . . . those *other* toys?" Victor asked.

"They and I serve the same master," Jagg said. "And our master will eat you alive if you don't get out of my way."

"The Devil doesn't scare me," Victor said. "Until tonight, I didn't even *believe* in him!"

The elephant, cat, and rabbit were lifting the bear off the puddled pavement.

"We've got to get him to Mrs. Shannon," said the elephant. "Maybe she can make him live again."

"The police will be here in a minute," Jagg said. "The toys will have to pretend to be just toys then, and the cops will think you stole them from the department store. They won't let you go to Mrs. Shannon's or anywhere else."

Victor kicked the suitcase, overturning it and spilling hundred-dollar bills across the pavement. "And what will the police have to say about all this money? Can you explain where you got it, Mr. Jagg? Do you think they'll let you go anywhere, either?"

Fear shone in Jagg's vicious eyes, which usually had room for no emotion but hatred. Victor suspected that the man had spent time in prison before and did not want to return.

"I'll kill you, Bodkins."

"Go ahead. Try," Victor said, standing up to him. "The police will arrive just in time to find you crouched over my body."

Jagg hesitated. He made a thin, unhappy sound, then hurriedly began gathering up all the scattered money, trying to return it to the suitcase before the cops arrived.

Victor stooped in front of the Oddkins and said, "Climb aboard, little ones. We've got to get out of here fast."

The cat and the rabbit scrambled onto Victor's shoulders and held on tight to his suit jacket. The elderly creature sat with his legs around Victor's neck; with his gloved hands he gripped Victor's rain-soaked hair. Victor put the elephant under one arm and the dog under the other, then tenderly picked up the lifeless, sagging teddy bear.

"Do you know the way to Mrs. Shannon's toy shop?" the rabbit asked anxiously.

"Oh, *that* Mrs. Shannon!" Victor said. "Yes, of course, she has been selling

Isaac's toys for years. I think I've passed her shop a few times. It's in the neighbor-hood.''

With the police sirens no more than a block away, Victor left Nick Jagg with the soggy stacks of money. He ran very fast along the alley, even faster than the wind which tried unsuccessfully to catch him.

19.

The utility company ran its electrical lines through the city's storm drains. One of their junction boxes was shorting, throwing bright, colorful sparks onto the stone walkway beside the water channel.

Rex's tuxedo was so wet that the sparks were extinguished when they struck him. He was in no danger of being set afire.

In fact the thing that concerned him was not the sparks but what the sparks revealed. In that flickering light a pack of large, vicious-looking rats blocked the way ahead. Their silvery whiskers bristled. Their white teeth gleamed. Their red eyes glinted with reflections of the sparks.

Rex knew that rats would have no desire whatsoever to eat a wooden marionette. But for a moment he was nevertheless afraid of them.

Then he realized that those filthy vermin were not threatening him but almost seemed to be bowing to him, as if they were servants. They were utterly silent and exhibited none of the frenzied behavior of ordinary rats.

''Ah,'' Rex said. ''I'll bet my master sent you. Did he not? You come from the Dark One.''

The rat at the head of the pack rose onto its hind feet, and Rex was not surprised when it spoke. Its voice was small but so shrill that it made Rex wince, a high-pitched yet harsh voice: ''We were sent by He Who Rules Below. Your master, our master, and the Master of All Evil. He wishes you to join him, and we will show you the way.''

"Lead on," Rex said.

The rats swarmed around him, and he accompanied them away from the sparking junction box, down the sloping storm drain, into ever deeper darkness.

"I'm sure the Dark One wishes to give me a new squad of toys to battle the Oddkins."

"Is that what you think?" asked the leader of the rats.

"Oh, yes. My first team failed me, you know."

"Is that true?"

"Yes, yes," Rex said. "Weasel, Gear, Lizzie, and Stinger—none of them had enough hatred in him to get the job done. None of them was strong enough or nasty enough to be of any real help to me. I had to try to do it all myself."

"How hard that must have been for you," said the rat.

They were walking in total darkness now, heading down, down, down. Even though he possessed excellent night vision, Rex could not see where he was going. He allowed himself to be guided by the pressure of the rats' bodies at his sides and behind him.

"My master will want to give me the best soldiers this time, the most ferocious demons to assist me," Rex said.

"I'm afraid that's not the case," said the rat. "Your master believes you have failed."

"But I haven't!" Rex cried. "My troops failed *me*. If I had been given better assistants—"

"The Master feels we have lost," said the rat, "and that the new toymaker will be Mrs. Shannon rather than Nick Jagg. So he wants you to be brought before him."

Suddenly, for the first time in his existence, Rex was afraid. "Not . . . no . . . wait . . ."

"We must not hesitate. Our master awaits us."

"But I destroyed the bear. I cut the magic life out of the bear!"

"But only the bear. You stopped only one of six."

The rats carried him onward and down, down. . . .

After a long while, Rex dared to ask, "What will my master do to me?"

"Oh," said the rat, "he won't tear you limb from limb or set fire to you and reduce you to ashes. Nothing like that. He just wants you beside him forever."

"But . . . that would be an honor!" Rex said happily. "To be at the Dark One's side, his companion. An honor indeed! So the Dark One must realize that even if I failed at this task, I am still a most valuable creation. He must realize that I am wonderfully evil and eager to serve him, for otherwise he would not want me always close at hand."

"Close at claw," the rat corrected.

"Yes, of course."

"Well," the rat said as they continued downward in blackness, "I'm afraid it's a bit different than you picture it. The Master wants you at his side, yes, but from now on you'll always have strings attached to your head and limbs."

"Strings!" Rex said, shocked. "But I am independent. I am not like other marionettes. I am without strings. I do what I want and go where I want."

"No more. You will be unable to make even the slightest movement except when the Master pulls on your strings. You will be forced to do anything he wishes, regardless of how humiliating and humbling the task. You will be totally controlled. You will never again lead but will always be led. You will be forever dangled in front of those who approach the Dark One's throne and will be used as an example of what happens to those who fail to do the Master's bidding. And all those who see you will be sickened by your condition, for you will have no pride, no dignity, no respect, and there will be no hope of ever being released from your suffering."

Rex tried to turn and run.

The rats seized him, held him, and carried him down into the deep, dark, stinking depths of the earth.

20.

In the alleyway behind the department store, one policeman held a gun on Nick Jagg while the other officer opened the suitcase.

The revolving red beacon on top of the squad car made the falling sleet look like drops of frozen blood. It cast waves of crimson light across the bundles of cash in the suitcase.

Squinting up at Jagg suspiciously, the officer said, "Where did all of this money come from?"

"It's mine," Jagg said nervously.

"But where did you get it? Did you steal it from the department store?"

"No! If you check, you'll find they're missing no money. Their safe is intact."

"Then where did you get it? Are you rich? What line of work are you in?"

Jagg said nothing more. Soon, when they ran a computer check on him, they would learn that he had been released from prison only that morning. They would learn that his worldly possessions at that time had consisted only of the clothes on his back and one hundred dollars. They would insist on knowing where he had gotten all this cash. He could not tell them that the Devil had given it to him. He could not tell them anything that would make sense. Finally, they would find an unsolved theft and convince themselves that Jagg had been the thief and that the money in the suitcase was criminally obtained. For the next few weeks or months, he would sit in a city jail, unable to post bail, and eventually he would be tried, convicted, and returned to prison.

He sighed and said, "I really wanted to build nasty little toys. It would have been so much fun."

5

THE NEW
TOYMAKER

1.

Worked into a stained-glass window above the heavy oak doors was the word WONDERSMITH, the name of Colleen Shannon's toy shop. The same word was painted across the large, arched display window in the stone wall to the right of the entrance.

With Patch, Skippy, and Gibbons still riding on his shoulders and head, with Butterscotch under one arm and Burl under the other, with Amos's ruined body held tenderly in one hand, Victor rang the bell.

The store and the apartment above it were dark. The hour was very late: three o'clock in the morning. Mrs. Shannon, who had lived alone since the loss of her husband years ago, would be asleep.

Victor was afraid that she had not heard the bell. He rang it again, then again.

"Is Amos showing any life?" Skippy asked.

"None," Victor said.

Burl said sadly, "Gibbons, you know the history of the Oddkins and the magic toymakers who produced them over the years. So tell us what we've all wondered for so long. What happens to an Oddkin when the life goes out of his body? What happens to his soul? What has happened to Amos's soul?"

"I don't know," Gibbons said, no longer gripping Victor's hair but holding on to his ears instead. "That was the one thing that Uncle Isaac did not tell me about our kind. I know everything else—but not what happens to us in the end."

Victor rang the bell again, and lights appeared on the second floor, above the shop.

"I have a theory," Skippy said. "When the life force goes out of one of us, when he becomes just another stuffed-toy animal, then I think his spirit goes to Heaven just like a human spirit. I mean, after all, God must like toys as much as everyone else does. Right? So what I figure is, we go to Heaven where we play with God and give Him pleasure for all eternity."

"That's a lovely thought," said Butterscotch.

The other Oddkins agreed.

"I hope you're right," Burl said. "Oh, I hope that's where poor Amos is now."

"He was a good bear," said Patch.

"A very good bear," said Gibbons. "There will never be another like him."

A woman's face had appeared at a second-floor window.

Victor stepped back from the door and waved at Colleen Shannon, hoping she would recognize him though they had met only a couple of times over the years. On his shoulders, Skippy and Gibbons and Patch waved too. From under Victor's arms, Burl waved and Butterscotch wagged her tail.

Mrs. Shannon stared down at them for a long moment, then turned away from the window.

"She's coming," Victor said. "She'll be here in a minute, and we can get in out of this terrible weather."

2.

Mrs. Colleen Shannon stood at her workbench in the back room of Wonder-smith, where every day she spent time repairing many of the toys that children brought to her "hospital." Victor Bodkins stood at her side. The limp bear lay in the middle of the bench, and the five living Oddkins stood sorrowfully around their lost friend.

They had told her everything that had happened to them, and old Gibbons had explained that she had been chosen to be the next magic toymaker.

"If you accept the job," Gibbons said, "you will receive the power that Uncle Isaac had, and you will be able to make magic toys of your own to help children in need."

Tears tracked down Colleen Shannon's cheeks. Though she had not known Amos the bear, she was saddened by his death; however, that was not why she was crying. She wept because all of her life she had loved children and had wanted to make their lives happier. Her own husband had grown sick and died soon after they were married, and she had never had children of her own. She was thirty-five years old now, and sometimes her life seemed lonely because she lacked a family. But this was the end of loneliness. From this day forward she would have the company of the living toys she made, and she would be comforted by the knowledge that her magical creations would help hundreds and perhaps thousands of special children in their time of greatest need.

"Oh, yes, Gibbons," she said, "I accept the job. I will be the new toymaker, and I promise to do the best job I can."

"I know you will," said Gibbons, putting one finger alongside his snout. "I know you will."

Colleen felt a sudden change in herself, a great warmth, and she knew that the toymaker's powers had just been transferred to her.

Victor said, "Mrs. Shannon—"

"Call me Colleen," she said, using a tissue to blot the tears on her face.

"Okay. And call me Victor. What I was wondering . . . well, you are clearly surprised by all of this, by meeting living toys, but you don't seem as surprised as I thought you would be."

"No," she said. "Because of . . . Binky."

"Binky?" Victor said.

"Who's Binky?" Skippy asked. "Sounds like a Las Vegas comedian to me."

"Wait here," Colleen said. She turned and ran from

the workshop, as light on her feet as any young girl. She hurried upstairs to her bedroom, grabbed Binky from his place on the bureau, and rejoined the others. "*This* is Binky," she said, putting the old stuffed-toy lion on the workbench.

The Oddkins examined Binky with interest and looked knowingly at one another.

Colleen said, "My mother died when I was only seven years old. The week before she passed away, she gave Binky to me. When Mother was gone, I was very sad and confused for a long time, but I got through those bad months with the help of Binky. I talked to Binky a lot, and he helped me to see that life must go on no matter what. He convinced me that there would be happiness ahead of me if only I did not let my mother's death depress me too much for too long. Binky was my special friend when I desperately needed one."

Watching her solemnly, the Oddkins all nodded.

Colleen said, "Of course, you see, when I grew up, I believed that my talks with Binky and our play together were just figments of a child's active imagination. But in the back of my mind, I guess I never quite gave up the idea that my Binky had *really* been alive. And that's why I'm perhaps not as surprised as you would have expected, Victor."

Gibbons put a hand on the lion's head. "Yes, he was one of us, all right. Made by Uncle Isaac in the early days. And judging by what a fine lady you've become, I'd say Binky did his job very well indeed."

3.

Like his friends, Burl wanted Mrs. Shannon to try to repair Amos and bring the bear back to life before fixing the others. "It's too terrible to see him lying there, just another toy, and a broken toy at that."

"Burl," Colleen Shannon said, "I'm afraid I can't do anything for Amos. His mission was completed, so maybe his allotted time on earth is over."

"But he never had his chance to help a special child," said Butterscotch. "And that's what he was made for, just like us."

"He helped countless children," Colleen said gently, "by leading you here to me and by preventing that Mr. Jagg from becoming the new toymaker."

"But he didn't get a chance to help his one *special* child," said Skippy.

"Nevertheless," Mrs. Shannon said, "I will start by repairing those of you who are still alive. You, too, must have a chance to help your special children, and you can't do that until you're made whole again."

Burl sat on the workbench beside Amos, one hand on the silent bear's shoulder. He watched with interest as Colleen took thread, materials, needles, and other tools from various compartments in the shelves and cabinets above the bench.

She put on a green workshop apron and repaired Butterscotch first, replacing the few scraps of cotton stuffing that had come out of the dog's leg. Victor threaded a needle for her, and she carefully stitched up the tear that had been the work of an alley cat. She cut a new ear for the dog from a piece of brown corduroy.

"I don't have material to match your other ear, but this will look darling. Besides, your corduroy ear will be like a badge of honor to remind us of the sacrifice you made by helping your friends bring me the news of my selection as toymaker."

"I'll wear it proudly," Butterscotch said, lowering her eyes shyly as Colleen sewed on the new ear.

Burl was surprised and delighted to see that their new toymaker had a sense of humor, too. Instead of giving Skippy a new powder-puff tail to replace the one that Rex had cut off, she sewed up a padded five-point star and stitched it to the rabbit's bottom.

"You won't ever have your star on Hollywood's Walk of Fame," she told Skippy, "because that's not your mission in life. But you *will* have a star because you deserve one."

With the help of a long-handled vanity mirror that Victor held for him, Skippy examined his star-shaped tail and was delighted.

"It's terrific!" Skippy said. "Better than a star on the Walk of Fame. I'd have to go to Hollywood every time I wanted to see my star there, but I can carry this one with me and look at it any time!"

To Patch, Colleen Shannon said, "You get your name because of the coloration of your fur, but why not give you a real eye patch like some wounded, one-eyed cavaliers had? It would be a mark of what a courageous fighter you are."

"Okay," Patch said, "but could I get washed up, too, and have my torn trousers repaired? And could my hat be cleaned and given a better shape?"

"Oh, yes, all of that," she promised. "But not tonight. We'll just do major repairs tonight, and tomorrow we'll clean you up."

She cut a circle of plaid fabric and stitched it to Patch's face where his missing eye had been. In the very center of the patch she sewed on a green button the same shade as his good eye.

"You'll be able to see as well from the button as from your glass eye," she said, "but it'll be more dashing."

Taking a look at himself in the mirror that Victor held, Patch said, "Oh, but it *is* dashing, isn't it? Look, Burl. Look, Skippy. Doesn't it give me such style? Anyone seeing a cat with such an eye as this would surely think, 'Ah, there goes a cat who has had great adventures, who has done much, who is a champion and survivor.' The ladies will swoon, and the kittens will stand in awe of a cat with such a patch as this!"

Burl watched—and giggled—as Colleen replaced Gibbons's burnt-off white hair with a mane of frizzy orange fuzzy stuff.

"You need colorful hair to make you look cheerier," she told the scholar.

"I'm young again!" Gibbons said, studying himself in the mirror. "Not as dignified looking, perhaps, but definitely younger."

Next to Amos, Burl had the most terrible wounds, and by the time Mrs. Shannon came to him, he was curious to see what peculiar new look she would give him.

Colleen selected a blue-and-white-striped material for his new trunk. She sewed it into a tube, stuffed it with cotton, and stitched it to his face.

"And how about a red and white polka-dot ear?" she said. "With such a trunk and ear, everyone will know you are no ordinary little elephant but something special, something very special indeed."

Skippy took the long-handled vanity mirror from Victor Bodkins and held it so Burl could look at his striped trunk while Colleen fashioned his colorful new ear.

"Hmmmmm," Burl said, "not bad. Though with this look, there's no way I'll ever fit in with a herd of real elephants on the veldt."

"But your special child will love you all the more because of the way you look," Mrs. Shannon said.

"Then that's good enough for me," Burl said.

Colleen gave him his new ear. He found that both that polka-dot-covered flap and the new trunk worked as well as the old ones.

"Heroes, every one of you," Mrs. Shannon said, "and your fancy repairs are your badges of honor."

She hugged them, one at a time, and Burl had never felt better than when he was held tightly in Colleen Shannon's arms.

"And now Amos," Butterscotch said. "The most heroic of us all. Help Amos, Mrs. Shannon."

"I'll try," she said, frowning. "But it's going to take time."

4.

While Colleen Shannon worked lovingly on the ravaged bear, Patch and Burl wandered around the cozy toy shop, exploring the place with interest, trying to take their minds off the major surgery being conducted in the back room. They came to an ornately carved cabinet in which were displayed a lot of antique toys that Mrs. Shannon had restored to their original condition and luster.

"Butterscotch is right," Burl said.

"About what?" Patch asked.

"About everything," Burl said. "But especially about how unfair it is that other toys never have a chance to know what life is like. Remember what she said in the department store when she saw those ordinary stuffed-toy animals? Unfair. And it is. Because all toys, even those not living, bring joy to children, and it seems as if they ought to have a bit of fun themselves."

"Maybe they do live in their own way," Patch said. "If the child believes his toy lives, if he believes it strongly enough, then who's to say it might not be true? A child's imagination is a wonderful thing, a pure and innocent thing, and maybe it can work a certain magic of its own."

A couple of minutes later, they were still staring at the toys in the case when Skippy ran in from the work room to tell them that Colleen Shannon had almost finished with Amos. "She's just got to sew up his restuffed belly."

They returned to the other room and allowed Victor to lift them onto the bench. The five living Oddkins watched anxiously as Mrs. Shannon completed the repairs on their friend and leader.

Amos's blue sweater—with its Alpha and Omega symbol—and the body under it had been slashed in several places. Colleen Shannon had used scraps of brightly colored cloth—green, red, yellow—to cover those gashes and to give the bear his own badges of honor.

But after she pulled the last stitch, tied the last knot, and broke the thread, Amos did not move. His eyes remained blank. He was not revived.

"Amos, please," Butterscotch said, "speak to us."

"Sit up and smile that furry, bearish smile of yours," said Skippy.

"Please," Burl said, "sit up and say 'Okeydoke.'"

But Amos did not return to life.

Beside the bruin's body was a pencil stub and a piece of paper on which were lines of poetry.

Sick with grief, Burl scanned the lines and said, "But . . . this reads like the work of Rupert Toon."

"I found the pencil and paper in the pocket of his sweater," Colleen Shannon said. "Who's Rupert Toon?"

Burl looked solemnly at his friends, and it was Butterscotch who finally had the courage to put into words what all of them now realized. "There was no Rupert Toon," she said. "Never was. The poems were all Amos's own, and we never knew. We made such fun of poor Amos's poems."

"Now," Skippy said, choking on his grief, "I'd give anything to hear him reciting Toon's lines again."

"Anything," Gibbons agreed.

"I feel so ashamed," Burl said, "of how we mocked that poetry."

"Sometimes," Patch said, "you can hurt another person's feelings without knowing it, just because you don't take time to think."

For a moment they were silent with surprise, but then they sobbed quietly for their lost friend.

Burl saw that Mrs. Shannon was weeping again and that Victor was crying too. The man put his arm around the woman, and she leaned her head against his shoulder.

She said, "I guess my new magic power can't bring him back if he's not meant to live again."

They stood staring down at Amos's body for a long while before Burl saw that Butterscotch was chewing at her recently repaired leg, tearing open the stitches.

Colleen Shannon noticed too. "Butterscotch, what are you doing?"

"I think . . . maybe . . . if I give some of myself to Amos. . . ."

"What do you mean?" Mrs. Shannon asked.

"Uncle Isaac filled Amos with magical stuffing. But he was *re*filled with ordinary stuffing," Butterscotch said. "Maybe that's why he can't come back to life."

"But I put his new stuffing into him," Mrs. Shannon said, "and I've got the magic now, so the cotton I use should be magical too—shouldn't it?"

"It'll be magical with the new toys you make," Gibbons said. "It'll give them life, of course. But maybe it isn't magical for old toys like us who were made by a previous toymaker. Maybe the only way we can bring Amos back is to give him some of our *own* stuffing—sort of like a transfusion of his blood type."

Butterscotch said, "There's nothing more magical than the love that exists between friends. Nothing finer or more powerful. When we give Amos a small portion of our stuffing, a little piece of ourselves, we'll be giving him love, and maybe love can make this miracle work."

Without another word from anyone, Colleen Shannon and Victor Bodkins helped the five living Oddkins by cutting their fabric to reveal their cotton innards. Then Butterscotch, Gibbons, Skippy, Patch, and Burl plucked out small pieces of their own stuffing and, one by one, inserted those bits of cotton into a slit that Mrs. Shannon made in Amos's belly.

Amos did not move.

Burl wished with all his might that Amos would come back to them. He wished so hard that his ears curled and his new striped trunk began to roll up.

Amos did not move.

Butterscotch gave a bit more of herself.

So did Patch. So did Burl. So did Skippy and Gibbons.

The workroom was as still as a churchful of people engaged in silent prayer.

Amos blinked. He yawned. He lifted his head and looked around the workshop. He said, "Was I hibernating?"

Full of joy and relief, everyone laughed. Colleen Shannon was both laughing and crying, and Victor said, "What a wonderful night!"

6.

Mrs. Shannon had stitched up the cuts that had been made in all the Oddkins to make possible their transfusion of stuffing and love. Now Amos stood on the workbench with his companions. After hugging each of his friends several times, he said, "This moment reminds me of a poem by Rupert Toon."

"Let's hear it!" Skippy said.

"By all means!" Burl said.

"Rupert Toon is our favorite poet," Gibbons said.

Butterscotch and Patch agreed.

Startled, Amos said, "He is?"

"Absolutely," Patch said. "Our very favorite poet. There is none other like him."

"That's for sure," said Skippy.

Amos grinned and said, "Then you're going to love this poem. I think it's one of Toon's best."

Moving to the center of the long workbench, he threw back his shoulders, pushed out his chest, held his head high, and recited the lines:

> Good food is nice, so people say,
> and cows are very fond of hay.
> Pretty clothes make you feel good,
> and termites have fun with wood.
> Money is a pleasure, I suppose,
> and a gardener may love a rose.
> But real happiness in life depends
> on having true and faithful friends.
> Riches, fame, interesting studies
> —none are half as good as buddies.

" 'Interesting studies'?" Skippy said.

Burl thumped the rabbit on the head.

"Oh, uh, wonderful!" Skippy said. "Brilliant!"

"Bravo!" Burl said.

All the Oddkins applauded, as did Victor Bodkins and Mrs. Shannon.

"Gee," Amos said, "if you really liked it, I've got another good one—"

"Oh, not two at once!" cried Patch. "No, no, that would not give us time to savor and enjoy the first one."

"That's right," Gibbons said quickly. "Give us a day or two to think about the first poem, Amos. We need time to savor it, to let it sink in, to enjoy it to its fullest."

"Yes, a day or two," Burl said. "Maybe even three or four days."

"Maybe a month," Skippy said. "It might take us a whole month to fully absorb and appreciate the first poem."

"It was that good?" Amos asked.

"It was the most amazing thing," Skippy said.

"It was . . . like nothing else," said Butterscotch.

"It was very much what it was," said Burl.

"Please," Patch said. "Give us time to think about it and enjoy it, Amos."

Amos grinned and nodded. "Okeydoke."

7.

Colleen Shannon said, "By the courage and determination that all of you exhibited in making the long journey from the toy factory to my shop, you have earned a special reward."

"Reward? My own TV show?" Skippy wondered.

"Our own library cards?" Amos suggested.

"A thorough dry cleaning?" Patch asked.

"Oh, it's a much better reward than any of those things," Colleen Shannon said.

She drew two stools up to the workbench and indicated that Victor Bodkins should sit on one of them. She removed her green shop apron, hung it on a wall peg, and took the other stool. When she asked the Oddkins to gather around, the six toys sat in a semicircle on the workbench in front of her.

"The moment that I agreed to become the new toymaker, I felt a wonderful, warm power enter me."

"Your magic gift," Gibbons said.

"Yes," she said. "I felt myself *filled* with magic power. But understanding and knowledge came to me as well. I suddenly knew everything there was to know about the history and the destiny of the Oddkins. Among other things, I know what happens to an Oddkin when the life goes out of its toy body, after it's finished serving the special child that it was made to serve. And if you want to know, I will tell you what will happen when you die. That will be your reward—the comfort of knowing what is to become of you."

The six Oddkins stared at her in amazement, and suddenly all of them spoke at once: Yes, oh, yes, they wanted to know whether they would get to serve their special children, whether they would go to Heaven like people or to some other place for toys with souls, yes, they just had to know, they were just *bursting* to know.

"I want to know, too," said Victor. "What happens to them? It better be something good. They deserve something good."

Looking slowly from one of their small, sweet faces to the next, Mrs. Shannon said, "Each of you, even Gibbons, will be sold and given to a special child who will desperately need a secret friend. And each of you will succeed in helping your child. Then . . . when your child no longer needs your friendship and advice, your soul will depart your toy body . . . and you will be reborn as a real animal so you can experience the joy of being fully alive."

"Real animals!" Burl whispered in surprised delight. "You mean I will be reborn as a *real* elephant?"

"Yes. You'll walk the veldt. You'll lead a herd. You'll know what it's like to taste cool water and fine, rich grass. You'll get to sire baby elephants and see thousands of beautiful African dawns."

"And I will be a real bear?" Amos asked.

Colleen Shannon nodded. "You'll have a chance to know the great pleasure of roaming vast green forests and eating berries from the bushes. You'll experience the deep, deep rest of winter hibernation and the lovely, lazy awakening in the spring."

"Oh, the poetry of it!" Amos said.

"You'll be a fine bear," Victor Bodkins said, wiping at the moist corners of his eyes.

"And I get to be a real rabbit?" Skippy asked.

"Yes. You'll know the joy of great speed, for you will run far faster than you can run now. You'll feel the wind in your fur and the soft earth of the fields beneath your feet. You'll experience the tremendous comfort and coziness of the burrow and will have time to savor the intense flavors of the wild grass, weeds, and vegetables that you will find everywhere in plenitude."

"You make it sound better than performing in Las Vegas," Skippy said.

"It's much better," Mrs. Shannon assured him.

"And I . . . will become a real cat?" said Patch.

"Yes. All sleek muscles and shiny fur. You'll climb and explore to your heart's content. The night will belong to you because you will have the eyes of a cat and will see through any shadow."

"And me?" Butterscotch asked shyly.

"Oh, dear one," said Colleen, "you will be the beloved dog of a wonderful family, and you'll receive their affection all the days of your life. You will know the pleasure of sitting at your master's feet with the knowledge that he treasures you. You will have your litter of puppies, too, and a chance to use your special talent for mothering."

If Butterscotch's large, painted-glass eyes could have produced tears, they would have let out a flood now.

"And me?" Gibbons asked. "What animal will I be? I was told that I had been patterned after an animal that existed in a very distant age but died out many thousands of years ago. How can I be reborn?"

Colleen smiled and ruffled the old scholar's mane of new fuzzy red hair. "You get to be whatever animal you choose. Lion, panther, bird, whale, anything you wish."

"Of course," Burl said, "you'll choose to be an elephant."

Gibbons rubbed one finger along the side of his snout. "This will take a lot of careful thinking. So many possibilities . . ."

"Think on it all you want," Burl said, "but you'll end up choosing to be an elephant. I'll probably see you on the veldt."

Amos leaned forward and blinked at Mrs. Shannon. "Ummm, gee, I don't like to seem ungrateful. I'm happy to know we're going to get a chance to be really, *fully* alive. But now I'm wondering . . . what happens when we die again?"

"When your lives as real animals are finished, you will awake in your toy bodies once more—but not on earth. In a higher place."

They all looked wonderingly toward the ceiling and toward the sky that was out of sight beyond the roof.

"Up there," she said, "you'll stay forever at His side because, of course, He *loves* toys."

"I knew it!" Skippy said. "I just knew it!"

Later, shortly before dawn, the sleet turned to snow. Colleen Shannon, Victor Bodkins, Amos, Burl, Patch, old Gibbons, Skippy, and Butterscotch stood at the front window of Wondersmith, watching as the falling snow transformed the grimy city into a clean, white fantasy land. Though they were at the end of the night, everything was suddenly fresh and new.

"No one ever has to be afraid of endings," Amos said, "because there aren't any. No endings . . . just new beginnings. Isn't it a wonderful world? Isn't it a wonderful life?"